Ben to the rescue . . .

"My foot!" Jessica wailed.

As Ben tenderly took her right foot in his hand, he nearly recoiled. Blood gushed from the transverse arch. Just below her middle toe, an inch-long gash gaped open horribly.

"Careful," Ben urged. "You don't want to make it worse. What did you step on?"

Leaning over, Jessica reached into the sand.

"A knife?" Ben scooped Jessica up and carried her toward the parking lot.

"I think I'm dripping blood on your bathing suit."

"Don't worry about it," he said tenderly. "Am I holding you OK?"

"Perfectly," she said in a silky voice. "Were you ever in agony and ecstasy at the same time, Ben? I'd rather be here like this with you than dancing with any other guy."

On top of everything else, Jessica was a poet, Ben realized. He just prayed that the wound wouldn't mean an end to dancing. Or running. He shuddered at the thought of Jessica's proud, strong body compromised in that way.

She had to be all right! He broke into a run, her weight as light as a child's in his loving arms.

Bantam Books in the Sweet Valley University series
Ask your bookseller for the books you have missed

And don't miss these Sweet Valley University Thriller Editions:

SWEET VALLEY UNIVERSITY®

Sweet Kiss of Summer

**Written by
Laurie John**

**Created by
FRANCINE PASCAL**

BANTAM BOOKS
NEW YORK • TORONTO • LONDON • SYDNEY • AUCKLAND

RL 6, age 12 and up

SWEET KISS OF SUMMER
A Bantam Book / August 1996

Sweet Valley High® *and Sweet Valley University*®
are registered trademarks of Francine Pascal
Conceived by Francine Pascal
Produced by Daniel Weiss Associates, Inc.
33 West 17th Street
New York, NY 10011

ISBN: 0-553-56707-1

Published simultaneously in the United States and Canada

Bantam Books are published by Bantam Books, a division of Bantam
Doubleday Dell Publishing Group, Inc. Its trademark, consisting of the
words "Bantam Books" and the portrayal of a rooster, is Registered in
U.S. Patent and Trademark Office and in other countries. Marca
Registrada. Bantam Books, 1540 Broadway, New York, New York 10036.

PRINTED IN THE UNITED STATES OF AMERICA

OPM   0 9 8 7 6 5 4 3 2

To Justin DuVan

Chapter One

Jessica Wakefield watched her legs disappear as Ben Mercer heaped sand over her golden limbs.

"Oh no!" she cried in mock dismay. "Now I'll never escape!"

"I hope not." Ben reached over and kissed her softly. Then her legs swung free, scattering sand, and his laughter joined hers. Jessica couldn't remember the last time she'd laughed so much with a guy.

The hot August morning seemed to shimmer with possibility. No matter that her summer as a lifeguard had gotten off to an agonizingly slow start in the romance department. If any eighteen-year-old in America knew how to make up for lost time, it was Jessica.

Yes, today was going to be perfect. The sky was cloudless, the towering waves were a surfer's delight, and gorgeous genius Ben Mercer had kissed her twice before breakfast.

1

Wow, had things changed since Memorial Day weekend! Ben had come on strong the minute he'd met Jessica, but she'd initially regarded him with all the enthusiasm she felt for garlic slivers lurking among the leaves in a salad—agggh!

At first she'd fallen big time for head lifeguard Ryan Taylor, a six-foot-four enigma who bristled with authority and glistened with suntan oil. Although Ryan had made Jessica feel great about herself as a lifeguard, it was her twin sister, Elizabeth, he'd admired as a woman.

Ben had been there when Jessica's crush had turned into a crash, when she'd finally realized that Ryan would never be hers. No, it was Ben who was her destiny.

Now she knew that Ben's oversize T-shirt concealed rippling muscles. And the baseball cap hid crisply cut dark hair that she loved to run her fingers through. And beneath the hair lived and breathed a brain that was as clever about having fun as it was about aerodynamics and the origins of obscure words.

Not that he was a goody-goody. He just knew enough about the big picture of life to realize that people ought to be happy whenever and wherever possible.

His sweet and easygoing nature made him practically unique in Jessica's love life. She already had a tumultuous marriage to Mike McAllery behind her. Then her intense but short-lived relationship with a young professor, Louis Miles, had ended in his tragic death in a car crash.

But that was all in the past. Ben Mercer was here now. She'd had a satisfying summer as a lifeguard, with many saves to her credit. Lots of summer fun too, and the excitements of Labor Day weekend to look forward to.

Jessica sighed with contentment. Stretching out on the warm sand and looking up at the flawless sky, she felt like the luckiest girl in the world.

A squadron of planes circled high overhead. In perfect unison the pilots dipped the wings of their planes and headed briefly out over the ocean, then swung back toward the shore, as if they too, were saluting her perfect happiness.

Jessica quickly ran her fingers through her hair, fanning the long, silky blond strands into a halo around her head. Rotating her sleekly tanned shoulders, she minutely improved the fit of her sexy tank suit.

Once, at the beginning of the summer, Ben had teased her about looking fat in a certain swimsuit, but that certainly didn't seem to be his opinion now.

They'd spent the last hour on a secluded little stretch of Sweet Valley Shore, ten minutes north of the rambling Victorian house they were sharing with Jessica's identical twin, Elizabeth, and their friends Nina Harper, Winston Egbert, and Wendy Wolman. Ben gazed at her with frank admiration—and she knew she deserved it.

Jessica had probably gotten more exercise this

summer than all her other summers put together. Hours of running on soft sand and swimming through rough surf had definitely paid off. Her muscles were beautifully hard and defined. Her skin glowed. And she knew that her blue-green eyes gleamed with a new kind of pride that came with doing an important job well.

Of course it didn't hurt a bit that Elizabeth had for once in her life bought a sexy swimsuit. Naturally she'd let it languish in her tidy bureau because she hadn't found the nerve to wear it. And that left it conveniently available for Jessica. The suit was a one-piece, but its shiny aqua green spandex stripes showed off Jessica's curves to perfection.

Overhead, white smoke shot out from the planes as a mile-high capital *I* took shape in the sky.

"Skywriting! How totally cool." Jessica's blue-green eyes widened as *L, O, V,* and *E* materialized above them, each letter formed by puffs that looked like giant marshmallows. "I wonder who the lucky girl is," she added with a sigh.

"How do you know it's for a girl?" Ben asked.

"I just know," she said confidently. "It's—" She broke off with a little squeal as the planes puffed out a *J* and an *E*. "It's for me!" she blurted excitedly. "I love Jessica!"

Jumping to her feet, she waved her arms over her head excitedly.

Ben's mouth twisted into the lopsided grin she was learning to read very well. The more asymmetrical the grin, the more sardonic the words

4

that followed it. The pattern was so reliable, she'd given it a name last night—Ben's Biting Wit Index, or BBWI, for short.

The grin on his face right now practically reached his right eyebrow, it was so crooked. According to her calculations, that meant she was in for some choice sarcasm.

"Oh, right," he drawled. "Sure it's for you, Jess. And the sun rose this morning so you could have light to apply your mascara by."

She was so pleased with her own perceptiveness that she didn't have room to feel hurt. "An eight!" she cried triumphantly.

"An eight?"

"On the BBWI, remember?"

His big blue eyes kindled. "The Ben's Biting Wit Index—how could I have forgotten? Hmm, an eight out of ten," he added. "Not bad."

Suddenly he lunged toward her, mouth open and teeth bared in a hungry grimace that would have made Dracula shudder. "But it's nothing compared with Ben's Biting Bite."

Shrieking, Jessica dropped back down to the pillowy white sand. Instantly Ben dropped down beside her and pulled her into his grasp. She shrieked again as his mouth descended toward her neck. The sound was soon transformed into a murmur of contentment. He was just barely grazing her skin with his lips, about as far from a bite as a kiss could get.

Sheer bliss. Happiness and a half. And then she

5

looked over his shoulder and saw the name in the sky. *JENNY.*

Jenny? Jessica couldn't think of a single Jenny, Jen, or Jennifer at Sweet Valley Shore or neighboring South Beach.

Well, whoever this Jenny was, she had some nerve cluttering up everybody's sky.

Ben turned over onto his back and followed Jessica's gaze. His arm tightened consolingly around her, but somehow that just made her feel worse. She didn't want to be the object of pity.

Maybe the swimsuit wasn't so sexy after all, she decided. Leave it to Elizabeth to screw things up in the wardrobe department. Would she never understand that one of the sacred obligations of a twin was to shop for two?

"I bet skywriting's terrible for the ozone layer," Jessica declared in an indignant voice. She wasn't sure what exactly the ozone layer was, but she'd heard her sister go on and on about the evils of hair spray and how damaging it was to the environment.

Ben chuckled. "Is this the same Jessica Wakefield who has to be reminded to recycle her soda bottles? By the way, that isn't skywriting up there. It's sky typing."

"Yeah, right," she said disbelievingly. She sighed as the planes turned around and headed back up the coast, leaving the mile-high *JENNY* behind them. Where was a brisk wind when you really needed one?

"I'm not kidding," Ben went on. "Skywriting is an old-fashioned art form, with a solo pilot tracing out letters in script. This is the high-tech version. One of the planes has a computer on board controlling the show. That's why the letters come out in dot matrix form, as if there were a giant printer at work."

"Oh, who cares?" Jessica said crossly. She felt like a fool for having blurted to Ben that she hoped the writing was for her.

Ben was forever telling her that she was smarter than she thought she was, but she couldn't help being afraid that someday he would wake up to the reality that she wasn't exactly Ms. Einstein. After all, he went to the University of Chicago, a college renowned for its incredibly high academic standards. And he was a proud member of Mensa, the national club for certified geniuses.

Propping himself up on one elbow, the genius shot her an exasperated look. "What do you mean, who cares? Does it always have to be about you to be interesting?"

"I can't believe you said that, Ben. You know, everything doesn't have to be a lecture. School's out. This is summer vacation."

"Pu-leeze." Ben rolled his eyes. "Just because I had the temerity to mention something you didn't know about, that's a lecture? Oh, but I forgot, it's summer vacation—let's all turn off our minds and be superairheads. By the way, *temerity* means—"

Jessica jumped to her feet, sending a shower of

sand over Ben's dark hair as she did so. *Let the world think he has dandruff.*

"I'm not a superairhead," she snapped. "And I know what *tamar—temerity* means."

"OK, define it," Ben commanded coolly.

"It's what those surfers out there have way too much of." She pointed at a wet-suited trio who were hanging ten in the monumental surf. "Look at that wave coming in. It's huge."

"Twenty feet peak to trough, I'll bet," Ben said, shielding his eyes against the glare.

One of the surfers was lurching dangerously to the side, and Jessica knew that trouble was coming. "This is no time to measure waves!" Adrenaline jump-started her body. She broke into a run.

She was halfway to the water when the surfer lost his balance. The giant wave seemed to curl around and suck him in.

Jessica doubled her speed, pounding her feet into the gritty sand beneath them, and then dove into the icy water.

Hamburger Harry expertly shook the strainer basket full of fries, scooped out an extra-large serving of potatoes, and pushed the golden mound across the counter toward Winston Egbert. As the hot, greasy aroma wafted his way, Winston crinkled his nose in appreciation. A sensible guy would have grown thoroughly sick of fries after a daily diet of them, but Winston rarely pretended to be sensible.

He always felt right at home making people laugh, even at his own expense—which was why he was able to spend the summer as Harry's human hamburger. Dressed in a costume as hot as it was ridiculous, Winston marched up and down the boardwalk, advertising Harry's cuisine.

Winston's clowning had let him pay his share of the rent on the beach house. And the job had one other redeeming feature, besides the free french fries. It was six thousand miles from Europe. Which meant that his girlfriend, Denise Waters, didn't have to see him as a fast-food impersonator.

Denise was off in Europe, eating pâté, not hamburgers. One of the reasons Winston was slightly desperate about money was that he'd given Denise a very expensive gold bracelet, engraved with both their initials, in the hope that she would remember him fondly while she was living the good life.

He'd planned to be a lifeguard, like the rest of his pals from Sweet Valley University, but he'd flunked the tryouts. The irony was that he was probably in good enough shape now to make the cut. He rarely sat down on the job because it made the cheese look bunchy.

In addition to trekking the boardwalk endlessly, he engaged in sumo wrestling matches with Harry's chief competitor, Hot Dog Howie. What had started out as a real fight had turned into a repeated entertainment staged for the tourists.

"It's a great show. I love it," Harry was saying as Winston crammed a bunch of french fries into his mouth. "The trouble is, everyone's seen it already."

Winston's mind raced. It sounded as though Harry was trying to work up his nerve to cancel the gig.

"You know our motto," Winston said jauntily. "Twice is not enough. I mean, it's not like it's always the same show."

He turned to a table of Harry's regulars, four mustached retired pediatricians who religiously played poker every day over their lunch. "Hey, Docs, did you guys see the way I made Howie eat his own roll this morning?"

"Yeah, I thought I was going to have to perform a Heimlich maneuver on him," one of them said, laughing.

"Don't listen to him, Winston," Dr. Frankel said. "He's just upset because he bet Harry that Howie would win this morning."

"It was hilarious," Harry said. He turned to Winston. "I've made a nice little bundle betting on you. Though I don't know how you pack in so much junk food and keep your boyish figure," he added as Winston doused a fresh batch of fries with salt and ketchup. Harry ruefully patted his paunch. It made him look twenty-nine going on fifty. "I put on weight just smelling my own cooking. But you can eat and eat and eat. . . ."

Winston snapped his fingers. "Harry, that's it—

you've come up with our next million. An eating contest! The human garbage disposal, Winston Egbert, versus the world."

"Oh, yeah? How can I score? Even if the contestants pay for what they eat—"

"No, man. The money's in the betting. Back me and you're rich for life. Guaranteed! I can outpig any and all contenders." Winston licked his salty lips. "A tough job, but somebody's got to do it."

"Speaking of tough jobs—" Harry muttered.

The screen door banged and Winston turned around. In walked beautiful but perpetually sulky Rachel Max, the leader of the rival South Beach Lifeguard Squad. Three of her friends trailed closely behind her.

Delicate-looking Kristi Bjorn and short, balding Mickey Esposito were OK in Winston's book, but he couldn't say as much for Kyle Fisher, who never took off his fishing cap or put on a smile. Kyle seemed to have appointed himself Rachel's watchdog for the summer, ever on the lookout to prove his worth by barking or biting.

"So who's minding the store?" Winston quipped. "Is it safe to go in the water?"

"Hey, I just took off to have a hamburger," Rachel retorted. "Sweet Valley is the squad with a leader who's permanently out to lunch."

Ryan Taylor, the head lifeguard at Sweet Valley Shore, had disappeared after the Fourth of July weekend. He had the reputation of being a loner

11

and a drifter, and the whole Sweet Valley squad was losing sleep over his absence—especially Elizabeth Wakefield. Then again, Elizabeth had lost sleep over him even while he was around. Winston wasn't sure what had or hadn't happened between the two of them, but whatever it was had changed Elizabeth into a moody housemate and worrisome friend.

"I went to visit my folks in Tilton, and I saw Ryan in the Trail's End Pub there," Kristi piped up. "Looked as though he was working as a waiter."

Winston swallowed the lump in his throat. He had this theory about the two South Beach girls. If you put tall, dark-haired, sultry Rachel and petite, fair Kristi into Harry's milk shake machine, the resulting blend would resemble petite, dark Denise. Of course the concoction wouldn't be half as delicious as bubbly Denise herself.

"So what'll it be, gang?" Harry was asking. "Everybody's usual?" He tossed burgers onto the grill for Rachel, Mickey, and Kyle, then started assembling a tuna melt for Kristi.

"How do you do it, Harry?" Rachel asked. She leaned over the counter, her lace-edged sleeveless yellow top revealing her generous curves. As Harry's eyes widened, Rachel's voice deepened suggestively. "I mean, how do you remember what all of us like? Do you have a little black notebook somewhere?"

Winston almost choked on a fry. Rachel usually

treated Harry as if he were something yucky she'd stepped in. Now she was practically coming on to him.

The effect wasn't lost on Harry. He almost sliced his thumb instead of the tomato for Rachel's burger.

"Rachel, tomato, it's simple," he managed to say. Then he blushed furiously.

"Hey, watch the mouth," Kyle said. His dark eyes glowered. "Should I punch him out for you, Rache?"

"Not until after lunch," Rachel said lightly. "I'm starving." She reached out and touched Harry's hand as he was about to put the top half of the roll over her hamburger. "Oops, don't forget the lettuce, Harry."

"Rachel, iceberg, it's simple," Winston couldn't resist saying.

Kyle took a menacing step forward. "Hamburgers should be seen and not heard," he said.

"Cool it, Kyle." Kristi put a hand on Kyle's arm.

"Yeah, save it for the triathlon," Mickey said.

Winston hid his smile behind a fistful of fries. If there was anyone on the Pacific coast that summer who looked less like a triathlon competitor than Winston, it was Mickey. He seemed to amble through life in a good-natured daze. He was a sort of absentminded professor type, who always had a paperback book at hand. He'd even been seen smoking a pipe now and then.

13

Then again, Rachel, Kristi, Mickey, and Kyle had each made an impressive save this summer. Like their Sweet Valley counterparts, they were sure to go home with merit pay. Lifeguarding and having a good social life required two different sets of skills, Winston had learned over the last few weeks. The guy who was right there with the snappy comebacks at a party might have leaden reflexes when he sat in the big white chair on the beach.

"So who's going to win the triathlon?" one of the poker-playing doctors asked.

"South Beach," Rachel said instantly.

"Sweet Valley Shore," Winston said just as quickly.

"You looking for action, Doc?" Harry winked.

"Us look for action?" Dr. Frankel asked innocently. Then he chuckled behind his shaggy black mustache. "You bet we are. No disrespect, Winston, but my money's on South Beach."

"You do a great hamburger trot," Dr. Ephraim added from the other side of the table, "but you're not exactly built for speed, son."

"Come on, Docs," Winston protested. "I'm not even in the race."

"That settles it." Dr. Garcia slapped the table. "My money's on Sweet Valley."

"Thanks a lot," Winston said. "That's really touching."

"Harry, you giving odds on Sweet Valley?" Dr. Ephraim called out. He did one of his show-off shuffles, bridging the cards behind his head.

Harry's eyes brightened and Winston thought he could see dollar signs flashing in them.

"You should be giving the odds, Doc." Kyle flexed his gleaming biceps.

"He's right," Rachel chimed in. "We've got the swimmers, we've got the bikers, we've got the joggers."

"You've got the braggarts," Winston said with a snort. "Sweet Valley's going to leave you guys in the dust. Here's how good I think we are," he rushed on in a spasm of home-team pride. "I'll bet our merit pay against yours. Deal?"

Rachel shared a triumphant look with her friends. As she stuck out her hand to seal the bet, Winston remembered one little problem.

He wasn't on the squad.

The only merit pay he had coming was another ton of french fries. He'd just put his friends' summer bonuses on the line, and he didn't even have a stake in the outcome.

The odds were a hundred to one that he was in *big* trouble.

The wave was as cold and hard as steel, but Jessica angled her dive perfectly and slid through the wall of water. It was one of the things she had learned this summer. The trick was to let yourself go, be one with the water, almost fooling it into opening up for you.

On the first dive Jessica came up empty-handed.

15

Out of the corner of her eye she could see that Ben and their squadmate Wendy Wolman were racing toward her as the two surfers who had made it to shore gestured and shouted hysterically.

Taking a large gulp of oxygen, Jessica dove into the surf again. The water had a force stronger than anything she'd ever felt before, pressing against her ears, squeezing her temples hard.

The raging sea dragged her deeper, and she felt a surge of panic. Jessica reminded herself that Ben was on the way. She didn't have to worry because Ben would get her out of there, no matter how bad it got. But the surfer was another story.

Suddenly she glimpsed a wet shock of blond hair bobbing in the water a few feet away and set out with a few hurried strokes. But the surfer was caught up in a wave, and he drifted out of reach. Lunging toward him, Jessica managed to catch hold of the gaudy board that dangled from a lariat attached to his left ankle. With only a few seconds of air to spare, she got her arms around him and forced them both to the surface.

The surfer struggled in panic, pushing them both under as he grabbed onto her neck and shoulders.

"Jess! Hang in there!" Ben's words rang out over the crashing of the surf and the pounding of her own racing pulses.

With her last reserves of strength, Jessica propelled herself upward. As she broke the surface her hand reached for and caught the rescue buoy that

Ben sent spinning toward her as effortlessly and flawlessly as if it were a Frisbee. She slapped the exhausted surfer's hands onto the red rubber rim.

"Can't . . . hold," he mumbled.

"Can!" she sang back at him. She placed her hand on top of his, kicking furiously and pushing the buoy toward Ben and Wendy.

"C'mon, baby," she cooed into the surfer's ear.

Ben reached her first and they worked together in silence to bring the surfer back to shore.

Head lifeguard Nina Harper met them at the beach with towels and blankets. She stretched the surfer out facedown so he could vomit seawater without choking on it.

Jessica turned away and Ben came up behind her, enfolding her in a warm embrace. He didn't speak for a while, but the tremor in his arms and the look in his blue eyes spoke a volume of verse. Then he said a single word.

"Temerity."

"Mmmm," Jessica said, sagging against him.

"We will name out first daughter Temerity."

"Second," Jessica mumbled. "First is Airhead Junior. No, Superairhead Junior."

His arms tightened around her. "Superwoman Junior," he corrected her in the tenderest voice she had ever heard.

Jessica wanted to close her eyes and sink into a fantasy with him, but it wasn't time yet. She could hear the harrowing gasps of the surfer emptying his guts. Over the rough, wet sounds came the rising

17

wail of an ambulance siren, the sobs of the surfer's friends.

Easing out of Ben's protective clinch, Jessica moved back into the center of the action. Nina was kneeling over the surfer, holding his head, her beautiful dark face intent with concentration. Wendy was making notes on the form attached to the clipboard she had in her hands.

Jessica felt strangely detached. No disgust, no pity as the surfer heaved. It was almost as if they were all in a movie, playing their parts.

Even the emergency workers in the ambulance seemed surreal, with their swift, choreographed motions as they got the surfer onto the gurney.

But as the ambulance pulled away, reality rushed back in. The surfer could have *died* out there.

She could have died.

The realization struck Jessica and she began to cry, uncontrollable, wrenching sobs. As Ben gathered her close Wendy and Nina tactfully drifted away.

Ben kissed her tears, and Jessica wiped her nose on his towel. Nobody was looking.

"I'm sorry—" She hiccupped.

"Sorry? What's to be sorry about? You're the bravest, the most beautiful, and positively the most brilliant—"

She put a finger against his lips. "You know what, Ben? I really am an airhead. That's why I can do those rescues. Because it's about not thinking. If you think, it's all over. For me, anyway."

"Then maybe the true definition of brilliance is knowing when *not* to think," Ben said solemnly. "You look wiped out," he added with a note of concern. "Want to go back to the house and crash?"

Jessica didn't want to move an inch. "No. I just want to rest for a minute right here," she said, sinking down into the comfort of the warm sand.

Ben put a towel beneath her head. Jessica slowly closed her eyes and drifted into a relaxed state. Then she suddenly sensed a great commotion around her. She opened her eyes to find that Ben was running around dizzily, dragging a stick behind him.

Jessica shook her head in bewilderment. "Ben? What are you *doing*?"

He flapped his arms. "What do I look like?"

"A complete weirdo?" She giggled.

"Try again," Ben said. He put one finger on the top of his head and whirled around.

"A propeller."

"How about a propeller plane?" Ben hinted broadly. "As in an old-fashioned sky, um, sand-writing plane?"

Jessica stood up for a better view, and there were the proud words, huge enough for the whole world to see: *I LOVE JESSICA.*

Elizabeth Wakefield gazed down from her bedroom window. Her heart swelled with pride as she

19

recalled Nina's description of Jessica's magnificent rescue. Being a lifeguard had done wonders for her twin. The world was getting to see a Jessica who cared about more than guys and clothes. More important, Jessica was getting to see a new self reflected in the mirror.

Elizabeth wanted to run out of the house and hug her sister on the beach, but she knew that Jessica had what *she* really needed at the moment—Ben's adoring attention. Oh, why couldn't it have worked out the same way for Elizabeth when she'd saved that kid on July Fourth weekend?

Instead of kissing her and fussing over her, Ryan Taylor had lashed out at her. The kid had gotten into trouble on Ryan's watch, and Ryan thought that he should have made the save. He'd been distracted by Elizabeth and their unsettling attraction to each other, and he'd taken his eyes off the water to meet her searching gaze and questing lips.

Elizabeth had been facing the ocean, and she'd made the save. Despite the fact that the child had recovered from the trauma, Elizabeth and Ryan's relationship had taken a severe turn for the worse. Ryan had handed over his command to Nina, walked away from the beach, and not come back. The worst part was, Elizabeth hadn't really gotten to know him or figure out what they might mean to each other.

She sighed. She had a boyfriend, Tom Watts,

whom she loved deeply. But he was far away, spending the summer in Colorado. Still, she wondered if she would have been drawn to the mystery called Ryan if Tom had been living in the beach house.

Two months ago such disloyalty to Tom would have been unthinkable. Now, though, as she looked out at the infinite, shimmering ocean, her own code of ethics seemed childish. How could she ignore her intense and confusing emotions about Ryan?

All her assumptions about life and love were shaken and uprooted this summer. After all, the notoriously flaky Jessica Wakefield was totally together and the famously fabulous Elizabeth Wakefield was a mess of indecision. Anything was possible. The sun might rise in the west. A decent girl might be in love with two guys.

Elizabeth's best friend and floormate, Nina Harper, was in the same predicament, as Elizabeth knew from blurted late night confidences. Nina's boyfriend, Bryan Nelson, had backed out of his share in the beach house at the last minute in favor of a job on Capitol Hill in Washington, D.C. That was how his high-school buddy Ben Mercer had ended up on the first floor. Nina alternately pined for Bryan and resented his not being there. Meanwhile she had found herself drawn to Paul Jackson, a slick-looking African American guy who was Bryan's exact opposite—casual and carefree.

But at least Paul was *there*, Elizabeth thought

21

enviously. A member of rival South Beach Lifeguard Squad, he seemed to spend every spare minute at Sweet Valley Shore or on the boardwalk in between.

One of Elizabeth's loves was in Colorado, and the other might as well be on Mars.

As Elizabeth stood at her window and watched Jessica and Ben cling to each other, she smiled even while the tears streamed down her face. "Hold on to him," she whispered fiercely to the unhearing air. "Hold on and don't let go."

The words were for her sister, and they were for herself too. Herself and which guy, though— Tom or Ryan? Would she ever see Ryan again and get to answer the aching question? Or would this summer be an unfinished symphony, destined to haunt her forever?

Chapter
Two

The searing pressure in Winston's chest was getting hotter and stronger. "So this is what it's like to swallow a flaming sword," he muttered. "Or maybe I'm about to give birth to a boulder."

No one was there to appreciate his witticisms because he'd spent the last two hours avoiding everyone he knew. His housemates were going to beat him into bread crumbs when they found out that he'd bet their merit pay. Since this was not a fate he relished, he'd taken the scenic route home from Harry's instead of making his usual beeline across the beach or the main road that ran parallel to it.

Zigging and zagging, he'd wandered deep into the maze of quiet residential streets known as Sweet Valley Cove. The homes here were modest cottages, a far cry from the gaudy beach-front condos of the rich and famous, where he'd made a pest of himself during his ill-fated stint as a tour guide earlier in the summer.

Instead of breathtaking ocean views, heart-shaped swimming pools, and a Porsche in every driveway, the Cove boasted picket fences, swing sets, and five-year-old station wagons. Clutching his chest, Winston tried to pretend that the freshly painted yellow cottage just ahead was his. If he could only make it to the front door, his girlfriend, Denise, would catch him in her arms as he fell, and she would cradle him tenderly until the ambulance came. . . .

The pain stabbed him anew. What it most felt like, Winston decided, was that he'd somehow ended up with a bull inside his chest, trying to gore its way out.

Wait a minute. Wasn't that how his cousin Maxie had described his first heart attack? Stifling a panicky groan, Winston reminded himself that he was about half a century younger than Maxie, and he'd smoked only one cigarette in his entire life.

But maybe this was really it, the big one.

"Denise," he called out sorrowfully. "I can't believe I have to die without one last glimpse of your face. Put flowers on my grave, sweetheart. Gardenias," he added, spotting a profusion of the waxy white flowers. The thick scent reminded him of a high-school gym full of girls wearing prom-night corsages.

A single tear rolled down his cheek. A grin curved upward to meet it.

A slight case of death was just what he needed to solve his little problem! His friends would *have* to forgive the late Winston Egbert for wagering their merit pay.

He envisioned his funeral in perfect detail. Nina would look stunning in a black silk suit with matching black beads in her cornrows. But halfway through the service she would lose her composure and throw herself on his coffin. "You were a jerk," she would sob, "but you were *our* jerk. Good-bye, Winston. Keep the angels laughing."

Suddenly he belched. It was a rich, ripe belch from way down deep. As the echoes faded he realized the pain was almost gone.

Not a heart attack after all. Just plain old indigestion. He was going to live!

Still, he'd *almost* had a brush with death—which meant that his friends simply had to forgive him.

And to sweeten the odds, he bought as a peace offering a beribboned jar of mango preserves that a white-haired lady was selling from a card table in her front yard. Then he hurried home, whistling.

Ben opened *The Los Angeles Times* to the puzzle page. "Want to do it with me?" he asked.

Jessica flushed. Then she realized what he meant. "Oh, do the puzzle with you?"

"You're hilarious, Jess," he said. Putting down the paper, he leaned back into his corner of the couch and fixed her with a steady gaze. "Aren't I allowed to love you for your mind—at least at this moment? It doesn't mean I don't want you in other ways."

"You're allowed." Jessica really liked the way he talked—matter-of-fact but warm, direct but not too blunt. She paid him back by being direct herself. "Is it, you know, strange to you that I was married for about five minutes?"

"I don't mind that you have a past," he said easily. "As long as you're happy with the present."

"I'm very happy." She wiggled her toenail, which had been freshly painted bright pink, and nudged his bare right foot with her own. "I don't mind about you either," she went on. "About you and Rachel."

"That's good," he said. "But I mind about Rachel. I know guys who have warm and cozy feelings about their ex-girlfriends, but she's definitely not in that category. She was a mistake, Jess, plain and simple."

"Well, at least that makes us even," Jessica stated. "My marriage was a mistake with a capital *M*. I don't even know why I call it a marriage. Marriage is for grown-ups, and we were just two kids playing house."

Leaning forward and grasping her left hand, Ben tenderly kissed her ring finger—unadorned now. "Look," he said. "No tan line. It's as if the marriage never happened. You told me it was annulled, and that's what an annulment means. It's kind of like a time machine that goes back and makes things un-happen."

Tears sprang to Jessica's eyes. Ben was amazing! When he forgot to be sarcastic, he was just about the kindest person she'd ever met.

The two of them were stretched out on opposite ends of the big striped sofa that dominated the living room, their blue-jeaned legs twining under one of the afghans knitted by their landlady, Mrs. Krebbs. By chance they were both also wearing red T-shirts—but there the resemblance ended. Jessica's freshly shampooed blond hair hung over her shoulders in loose waves. Ben's dark hair was doing its imitation of a porcupine with a buzz cut.

Jessica felt incredibly safe, as cozy as a child playing house while the parents hovered just out of sight—but better yet, there weren't any parents around. Their four housemates were otherwise occupied. Nina, Elizabeth, and Wendy had gone grocery shopping. Winston was probably still hanging out at Hamburger Harry's.

The three-story Victorian beach house was exceptionally nice for a summer rental. The furniture was mismatched yet decent, and the confetti-pattern oval rag rugs pulled the assorted colors together. The high white ceilings and fluttery draperies added freshness, the rose-patterned wallpaper added faded charm, and who cared that it was peeling at the corners?

Although it had enough bedrooms to provide sleeping space and a shared bathroom for each of them—Elizabeth and Nina on the second floor, Ben and Winston on the first, and Jessica and Wendy in the attic—it was easy to imagine the house as a private residence.

It was, for instance, the kind of place an old married couple might spend their summers in. *Could we ever have a future, Ben?*

Instantly she chided herself for even thinking the treacherous words. *No, Jess. None of that. It's a summer romance. You'll be lucky if you ever see him again after Labor Day.*

"Jess, are you OK?" Ben's voice pulled her out of her daydream. "You're really something else. You're one of a kind, you know that?" He sealed the words with a kiss.

Jessica's lips tingled and began to part. Then she heard car doors slam. Out of the corner of her eye she saw Elizabeth, Nina, and Wendy coming up the walk.

One of a kind, she repeated to herself as Elizabeth came nearer. In the presence of her identical twin the words gave her a kind of guilty thrill.

The two girls had always been as different in personality as they were alike in looks, and yet they'd always thought of themselves as two of a kind. "Two sides of a complex equation with an equal sign in the middle," was how Elizabeth had once put it. "That's the Wakefield Theorem."

Could Ben disprove the theorem by becoming her other half, her truest partner? And was that

Jessica's deepest longing—or her darkest dread?

Ryan opened his wallet and pulled out the ivory business card. Below the raised letters of the name was a telephone number he knew by heart but never trusted himself to get right.

Elizabeth had once said that he didn't trust himself, period.

She'd tried endlessly to get him to see himself through her eyes, but what was the point? She saw an illusion. All the lifeguards did. Ryan the tallest, Ryan the strongest, Ryan the fastest. If only they knew the truth.

The young woman whose number he was dialing knew it, and that made everything both better and worse. He could relax—as much as he ever relaxed—and be himself with her. But without the fiction that he was some kind of god who could rule the waves of the ocean, he was a nobody. A nobody with pretensions, the lowest sort of all.

As if his life weren't complicated enough, the girl reminded him of Elizabeth. The resemblance wasn't physical. Although pretty, she was hardly a glowing beauty like the Wakefield twins. It was in character that she and Elizabeth were similar. They were both helpers, healers. Each of them, in her way, thought she could save Ryan Taylor—and both wanted to, the fools.

Blast it, he shouldn't have allowed himself to think about Elizabeth, not for a minute. He dialed the other girl's number.

*　　　*　　　*

Elizabeth shouldered open the screen door, then held it with her body so Nina and Wendy could get inside too. The girls had shopped big time, and each of them was toting two bulging grocery bags. For once, Nina had declared in her new authoritarian tone, they would manage to get everything on their list.

"Don't get up and help or anything," Elizabeth snapped at Jessica and Ben, who were stretched out toe to toe on the big living-room couch.

"Aye, aye, sir," Jessica retorted sarcastically with a sharp salute. She dug her feet into the cushions of the couch.

"Give us a second," Ben said mildly, standing up. He took one of Elizabeth's bags and one of Nina's and headed for the kitchen.

"Thanks," Elizabeth said as Ben set the bag down on a countertop. "Um, sorry I bit your heads off. The market was a zoo—checkout lines a mile long, and by the time we got to the car—"

Ben waved away the rest of the explanation. "Hey, no big deal. I wanted to come in here anyway and get Jess a fresh lemonade. Saving lives is thirsty business. Even more demanding than surfing the supermarket aisles."

He opened the refrigerator door and bent over. Elizabeth had to resist the impulse to kick him.

"You had it coming, Liz," Nina said softly as Ben wordlessly left the room to rejoin Jessica.

Wendy raised her eyebrows and busied herself finding space in the cupboard for three big boxes of cereal.

"Are the lovebirds getting to you?" Nina continued.

Elizabeth put milk and butter into the refrigerator. "I'm really glad for Jess," she said loyally.

"Of course you are," Nina agreed. "But that doesn't mean they're not getting to you."

As if to prove the point, the sound of giggles floated in from the next room. Elizabeth was all too glad to be distracted by Wendy's adopted stray dog, Paloma Perro, who suddenly streaked into the kitchen and gyrated around Elizabeth's ankles like an animated dust mop.

"Yes, yes, you'll get yours," Elizabeth muttered to the dog as he sniffed at her ankles and the grocery bag.

"And you'll get yours back in a couple of weeks," Nina said. "When you and Tom are reunited. So try not to let the green-eyed monster get you, OK?"

Elizabeth's face flushed in anger. Nina had become their squad leader when Ryan had defected, but that didn't mean she got to play den mother too.

"I'm not jealous!" Elizabeth stormed. "It's Jess's turn for a little happiness, OK? I just don't want her to get hurt, that's all."

"You don't think she and Ben are solid?" Wendy asked.

"Oh, sure—for the moment," Elizabeth returned quickly. "But Jess has a tendency to screw up when things get too easy."

"There's nothing shameful about jealousy," Nina insisted, apparently determined to hold on to the topic for dear life. "Being jealous is natural."

"So is arsenic," Wendy piped up.

"I am not jealous of Jessica," Elizabeth rapped out through clenched teeth.

It was just that Jessica's best-ever summer happened to coincide with Elizabeth's worst ever.

She couldn't believe how upside down and inside out it all was.

Jessica had been the darling of the lifeguard team, while Elizabeth had barely made the squad. Jess had snared a super guy, while Elizabeth had driven hers away.

With a sickening little lurch, she wondered if Jessica had been plagued by the sort of feelings toward her twin that Elizabeth was feeling now.

Resentment.

Jealousy.

"I'm jealous," she said to Nina in a teeny-tiny voice. "OK? Satisfied?"

Nina touched her lightly on the shoulder. "You're allowed to be human," she said. "Meanwhile we've got a bigger problem. This was absolutely, positively going to be the marketing trip to end all marketing trips—but we're out of jam. Jelly. Preserves. We got smooth peanut butter, crunchy peanut butter, and no-salt, low-fat peanut butter, but we forgot about the other half of the sandwich."

"We've got jealous but no jellies," Wendy said, an impish smile on her face.

Nina groaned.

Elizabeth could see why Winston had grown so close to tall, gray-eyed Wendy over the summer. The two of them shared a compulsive sense of humor, favoring practical jokes and truly terrible puns.

"Maybe the guy Jessica pulled out of the water will send her a big thank-you basket," Wendy said hopefully. "Fruits, nuts, candy, and some nice little jars of expensive jam."

Nina folded her arms across her chest and shook her dark head. "We're not going to hear anything from the guy Jessica saved. He's too big a loser to call or write or do anything. Sometimes I don't know why we're in the lifesaving business. It's definitely not for the thank-yous," she added emphatically.

Elizabeth's gaze drifted toward the window. When Ryan had been around, they'd all known exactly why they were in the lifesaving business, although no one had ever exactly put the feeling into words. It had seemed like the only game in town, the only real action. They'd been focused and fiercely dedicated.

If only Ryan had stayed, the summer would have been a dream instead of a nightmare.

And Elizabeth wouldn't have had to be jealous of her own sister.

Nina's voice broke into her thoughts. "Let's go talk to Jessica and Ben about Labor Day. I've got everybody's assignments. And we've got to talk about our triathlon strategy."

The triathlon was an annual end-of-summer competition between the lifesaving squads at Sweet Valley Shore and South Beach—and the mention of it provoked Elizabeth into another one of those sickening revelations about the state of her own soul.

Because not only did she want to outrun, outswim, and outbike Rachel and her crew, she wanted to outrace her own sister!

"And heeeeeere's Winston," Winston trilled gaily as he danced into the house.

"Winston, are you *drunk?*" Jessica demanded, squinting at him.

"*Moi?* Drunk?" He only wished.

His confidence in his friends' forgiveness had begun to erode as soon as he started up the walk to the house. It had evaporated totally when he came through the door and heard everyone animatedly discussing the triathlon.

"Winston, are you OK?" Wendy asked in a voice of genuine concern.

"I am not drunk," he said. "And I am not OK. Just kidding," he added.

His friends looked at him with more than their usual curiosity. Anyone would think he was behaving strangely.

34

"Actually I have some, uh, interesting news," he began. "I sort of, well, uh . . ." He gave a sickly smile.

"You did?" Ben said. "That's fascinating, Winston."

Jessica poked Ben in the ribs.

Winston looked from one face to another. "Er, I . . ." He reached into his backpack. "I bought you a jar of homemade mango preserves," he proclaimed triumphantly.

"That's great, Winston! Positively psychic." Wendy took the jar from his hand. "The one thing we forgot to get at the market." She admired the square of calico cloth tied around the lid with a ribbon. "Homemade jams are the greatest."

But Nina was folding her arms across her chest. "Out with it, Winston," she said. "How did you screw up this time?"

Winston looked at the ceiling.

Winston looked at the floor.

Winston looked at the front door and considered running all the way back to Sweet Valley University.

"It can't be *that* bad," Wendy said gently.

"Yes, it can." Nina's eyes were hard.

"She's right," Winston blurted unhappily. "It's the stupidest, silliest, dopiest—"

"Enough with the commercials!" Ben cried out. "Tell us."

"I bet everybody's merit pay on the triathlon," Winston said flatly.

The room went dead silent. Then, to his amazement, his friends started to laugh.

"Winston, that's hilarious."

"Oh, Winston, that's the funniest . . ."

But something in his eyes betrayed the truth, and one by one the laughter stopped.

Chapter Three

Wendy Wolman stifled a groan. Winston was her best friend at Sweet Valley Shore, a good-hearted joker who meant more to her each day, but this time he'd really gone too far.

Over the edge. In trouble, big time.

She didn't voice her thoughts, but she didn't have to. Her housemates were doing a swell job of letting Winston know that this time he was really in trouble.

Although Wendy couldn't join them, she couldn't blame them either. She looked at the stricken faces around her, and she saw a lot of dreams turning to dust.

Jessica seemed on the verge of tears as she clung to Ben on the couch. "It's all right for you, Winston Egbert," Jessica seethed. "Your girlfriend is rich. But Ben and I were planning to use our merit pay for plane tickets between Chicago and Sweet Valley."

Ben's arm tightened around Jessica. "There's always E-mail," he said encouragingly, but his blue eyes were downcast.

"It's the principle of it," Nina fumed at Winston. "You're not even on the squad! How could you? How *could* you?"

"I was going to use that money to protest human rights violations," Elizabeth said grimly, folding her hands across her chest. She angrily tossed her long blond ponytail. "You didn't just hurt us, you hurt a cause."

Winston put his hands over his eyes. "I killed human rights? Would somebody please shoot me and get it over with?"

He looked truly pathetic, Wendy thought. It didn't help that he was wearing one of his most ridiculous outfits either—baggy red plaid Bermuda shorts and a turquoise Hawaiian shirt. With his mop of curly brown hair, he looked like a clown from central casting. All that was missing was a honkable nose and a little car.

Wendy just couldn't help but soften toward him. After all, Winston was responsible for one of the most amazing twists in her life. He'd black-mailed Wendy's all-time fave singer, Pedro Paloma, into taking Wendy out for dinner. In exchange Winston had agreed to stop pointing out Pedro's fabulous condo to starstruck tourists. And Pedro had fallen in love with Wendy.

No matter that Wendy's mirror told the University of Nevada senior that she was plain. No matter that guys who weren't worthy of polishing Pedro's cowboy boots had passed her by in favor of curvier girls whose hair did something other than just hang there.

Pedro not only thought she was witty and clever, kind and brave, he thought she was beautiful. The gray eyes she'd always thought boring had even inspired his latest song, "The Girl with Smoke-Colored Eyes."

And she owed it all to Winston. She even owed her darling dog, Paloma Perro, to Winston. After all, the two of them had been together the night that the shaggy mutt had attached itself to her.

"Whoa. Back up, team. You're all missing the point," Wendy improvised indignantly. "Winston made the bet because he wanted to send a message to South Beach," she continued. "He thinks we're the best. He's so sure we're going to win, he'd stake anything on it. And you're mad at him? Gimme a break. That's what friends are for, believing in you no matter what."

"With friends like that, who needs enemies?" Nina retorted.

Wendy waved her hand dismissively. "Come on, Nina. You're our leader. It's time *you* expressed a little confidence in us. The truth is, you treat us all like screwups. But have we let you down yet?" She gazed challengingly at the squad leader.

Nina's black eyes flashed, and for a moment Wendy thought her career as a lifeguard was all over. Then suddenly the tension seemed to evaporate. Nina's shoulders visibly relaxed. Her voice softened.

"No," Nina admitted. "You haven't once let me down. In fact, you're about as good a team as anyone could ask for. I wake up scared every morning, praying that this won't be the day we lose somebody, but that's not because of you guys. It's me I don't have confidence in. I'm just not sure I'm cut out to be a leader, that's all."

The words came out in a rush, as though they couldn't wait to escape now that a door had been opened.

"The day Ryan handed me the whistle was the scariest day of my life," Nina said. "But I couldn't even tell you, Liz. I mean, I could hardly admit it to myself. I knew if I let on about my fears, we really would have a disaster. I guess that's why I hid behind the drill-sergeant mask."

"It fit you awfully well," Winston muttered.

Glaring at him, Elizabeth hugged her housemate and best friend. "You're a wonderful leader. Even when I haven't liked you this summer, I've loved you. And admired you."

"Have I been that unbearable?" Nina asked.

"Of course not," Elizabeth said.

"Come on, Liz," Wendy said. "She can take it. You've been completely insufferable, Nina. But you know what? Your instincts were right. It was better for us to focus on how obnoxious you were than on how scared we were when Ry—" Her voice faltered. "When you took over. Not that we didn't have faith in you—"

"I know," Nina said. "But I'm not Ryan."

"Speaking of Ryan," Winston said, "Kristi told me she saw him in Tilton. He's working as a waiter at the Trail's End Pub."

Wendy saw Elizabeth turn pale.

"Speaking of Kristi, are we really going to beat South Beach?" Nina said quickly.

"Hey, we've got to," Jessica declared. "Not just because of the money. Because of the way Rachel's bugged us all summer. She practically decapitated me with that Frisbee, remember? I'd like to pound South Beach into the sand."

"And what about the time they cut the rope on the No Swimming sign and Captain Feehan chewed us out because he thought we weren't doing our job," Nina contributed. "Let's hit 'em where it hurts."

"And I've got a score to settle with Rachel." Ben's tone turned bitter. "I'm still in debt because of her. She wanted jewelry for her birthday, and it had to be serious jewelry—sapphires. And she shamed me into taking her to restaurants where I couldn't even afford the parking. And then there were the loans, quote unquote, that she never paid back. She bled me almost dry. Boy, would I love to repay the favor."

"And the poisoned hot dogs," Wendy cried. "They could have killed my poor little Paloma Perro." Suddenly she gasped. "Oh no! Did we put the steak in the refrigerator before we came in here?"

Nina groaned.

Wendy put a finger to her lips, and they all cocked an ear to the kitchen. The sounds were unmistakable: butcher paper being merrily trampled, beef being dragged around the linoleum floor and slobbered over.

"Twenty-eight dollars and ninety-seven cents' worth of cut-to-order rib eye," Nina moaned. "To celebrate your save, Jess."

"Well, it's the thought that counts." Jessica blew Nina a kiss. "Thanks, Nina. But aren't you having dinner with Paul, anyway?"

"Not until late. I figured I'd hang out with you guys while you ate."

"Is the steak my fault too?" Winston asked piteously.

"Of course not," Wendy said.

"I'm going to make it right, anyway." He clapped. "Egbert's famous garlic-free 'kiss-me' pesto coming up."

"I'll make the salad," Nina volunteered.

"Make it do what?" Wendy asked, and everyone laughed. Everyone except Elizabeth.

"I'm sorry, I don't feel well—you'll have to count me out," she murmured. "Jess, congratulations. I'm so glad you're safe."

She fled up the stairs, leaving her friends gazing after her in dismay.

Wendy sighed. Just when she'd thought everything was calm *chez* Krebbs, Elizabeth had to go and have an emotional breakdown. About the hundredth she'd had that summer.

Well, Wendy had managed to pull Winston out of the fire, but someone else was going to have to save Elizabeth. The Wakefield twins were a mystery Wendy didn't quite understand. They were as changeable and unpredictable as the ocean currents. And their moods sometimes seemed almost as powerful.

Wendy couldn't wait until Pedro got back from his tour and pulled her out of the Wakefields' orbit.

Meanwhile, there was basil to chop. She followed Winston into the kitchen.

Elizabeth stood at the window, letting the ocean fill her eyes and her mind.

The waves were calm now, cresting and breaking with a musical *whoosh* sound, a very different Pacific from the one that had almost claimed a surfer just hours ago. A luminous thread of green meandered low in the horizon, promising a memorable sunset.

Her chest swelled with a feeling she couldn't quite identify. Painful and sweet at once, it was partly loneliness, but a kind of euphoric loneliness.

"Tom," she said aloud.

The name thudded dully against the rose-patterned wallpaper, then fell flat.

She loved Tom, and for the umpteenth time

she wished they'd spent the summer together. But he wasn't the one she missed. In a peculiar way he was right there with her and she with him, even though he was off in the mountains of Colorado at an intensive course in communications. They were almost beyond missing each other, so solid was their relationship. That awareness warmed her.

But there was no point in trying to kid herself. The bittersweet loneliness was about Ryan. Her light-headedness at Winston's news that Kristi had seen Ryan in Tilton was all the proof she needed. He was the one she missed, not because they had a great bond, but because they didn't.

Kisses you could count on the fingers of one hand, a glimpse or two of the vulnerable man beneath the tanned muscles—that was all that Ryan had given of himself. He'd spent their precious weeks together pushing her away.

At first she'd thought she was doomed to make one wrong move after another in his presence. She'd almost failed to make the lifesaving squad because she'd repeatedly tripped over her own feet when his hooded eyes were on her.

And while she'd hungered for his kisses, she'd felt completely incapable of igniting any sparks in him.

Then it had turned out that he was attracted to her too much, not too little. The revelation had burst out in a desperate, searching flurry of kisses in the lifeguard station that had almost ended in tragedy.

Then he'd disappeared, taking squad morale and Elizabeth's heart with him.

Nina had pulled the squad back together, but Elizabeth's heart was still in pieces. There were moments when she gave up on him completely. And moments like this, which were even more painful because they carried the burden of hope.

As she looked at the ceaseless ocean and the deepening sky above it, she felt a sudden rise of spirits. A surge of certainty that he had forgiven her.

She pictured him standing at a window somewhere in Tilton, yearning for her but still at war with himself—the man who loved to save lives but refused to take the responsibility for anyone else's happiness. The waves lapping the shore seemed to be coming from him, bearing a message. She half expected to see a bottle tossed up onshore. Inside would be a square envelope with her name on it.

But what would it say on the paper folded and refolded within the envelope? She couldn't read the writing, even in the piercing light shed by her imagination.

Did the words invite her to embark on a romance? Or did they once and forever proclaim Ryan the eternally solitary sailor, destined to float solo through the sea of life?

One thing was certain. She had to find out or spend the rest of her own life gazing out windows. Maybe their moment was behind them, but maybe it wasn't, and she owed it to herself to find out. Owed it to herself and to Ryan. And perhaps to Tom more than to anyone else.

Then she slid into a pair of ribbed black leggings. Shaking out her ponytail, she ran a brush through her long blond hair. In the mirror she was surprised to see a reflection of Nina, staring at her from the doorway.

"You OK?" Nina asked. She leaned against the doorframe, as though to send the message that she didn't intend to intrude on Elizabeth's space in any sense of the word.

"OK enough," Elizabeth said.

"Want to talk?"

"It's funny." Elizabeth put the hairbrush in her knapsack. "Back at school you and I talk about everything. But this summer it's almost as if we made a deal not to talk about the things that matter most. Like your doubts about yourself."

"And yours about you," Nina pointed out. "I guess in a way you could say Ryan did a number on both of us."

Elizabeth patted the bed, inviting Nina to cross the threshold. Suddenly she felt an urgent need to share her thoughts.

"What made him run away?" she burst out. "Why did he leave you with a job you were unprepared for and me with this—" At a loss for words, she turned her hands palms up and shrugged helplessly. "This Ryan-shaped question mark," she finally said.

"You got me." Nina sighed. "I never understood the man and I never will. He seems to have it all going for him, but he just can't deal with it."

"Does it have something to do with that kid who died on the beach last summer?" Elizabeth mused.

"I think that's a part of it. A secret, maybe."

The two girls looked at each other.

"Do I really want to know what he's all about?" Elizabeth asked wearily. "A moment ago I thought I did, but maybe I'm crazy. Maybe I should consider myself lucky he's gone away. Out of sight, out of mind," she added ironically.

"Yeah, right," Nina said. "You really want my opinion?"

"I *think* so."

"You don't have any choice. You've got to find out what's going on with Ryan before it tears you apart."

"Are you in the same confused state about Paul as I am about Ryan?" Elizabeth asked pointedly.

Nina's cheeks glowed. "Summer does weird things to the head. I love Bryan, but—" She tightened her lips and let the thought dangle.

"But," Elizabeth agreed. "The most dangerous word in the language."

She stood up and reached for the keys to the Jeep.

Pedro Paloma's basset hound, Carlos, greeted Wendy with a moist kiss, eager pawing, and a cacophony of barks.

47

"Why isn't he ever so sweet to me?" Winston complained. "Don't you love me, Carlos?" he asked, bending down to fondle the floppy, ticklish ears.

Issuing a single short bark, Carlos bolted out the open door and zeroed in on his favorite eucalyptus tree.

"You heard him," Winston said to Wendy. "That bark was unmistakable. 'No, Winston, I do not love you,' it said."

"Don't be silly." Wendy grabbed Carlos's leash from its brass hook next to the door, made sure that she had her key, then pulled the door shut, trying the knob twice to ensure that the door was locked.

"Are we paranoid or what?" Winston asked. "Nothing bad has ever happened on this street. The kids in these houses grow up zit-free. No one even burns toast around here."

"Yeah, it's nice, isn't it?" Wendy loved the condo Pedro was renting, with its red barrel-tile roof and the free-form swimming pool in a rock garden composed entirely of yellow flowers. "Not that your average person who lives fifty yards from the ocean needs a pool—"

"But it's nice," Winston agreed.

"And Pedro wants to keep it that way," Wendy said. Carlos barked at them, and she broke into an easy jog. "I think he feels more responsible than if he owned the house. Especially because the owner admires him and came way down on the rent.

the condo out to all his fans?"

"Boy, that was a lot of hamburger hours ago," Winston said. "Well, I guess he'll own his own fancy beach house pretty soon. What's the latest news from the tour?" He huffed a little and dropped a pace behind her.

"He must be working really hard because I haven't heard from him for a few days." Four— no, five days, to be exact, Wendy realized with a little lurch. "And then he's probably got a constant bunch of groupies surrounding him when he's offstage." She'd meant the last words to be a joke, but somehow they came out shakily.

"Oh, right," Winston said. "Let's face it, Wen. He's forgotten all about you. The fact that he gave you the key to his place and left Carlos in your care doesn't mean a thing. He especially doesn't think about you when he sings 'The Girl with Smoke-Colored Eyes.' "

Winston stopped, picked up a stick that had somehow been permitted to lie on the pristine front lawn belonging to one of Pedro's neighbors, and flung it. "Hey, Carlos, fetch," he said. He folded his arms across his chest and stood there, breathing hard.

Wendy looked at him incredulously. "Are you tired?" she asked. "Winston, we were hardly moving."

"And I thought I was in pretty good shape," Winston said unhappily. "Walking for hours every day in two tons of hamburger costume—that practically qualifies as weight lifting, doesn't it?"

"The heaviest thing you lift is a forkful of fries," Wendy admonished him. "It's a good thing you're not competing in the triathlon."

"You think I would have bet on us if I were in it?"

She swatted him. "The less said about betting on us, the better."

"Not to change the subject or anything, but why don't we put Carlos on his leash and go to the boardwalk?" Winston suggested. "You've shamed me into wanting exercise."

"Exercise on the boardwalk?"

Winston cleared his throat. "Er, pinball."

"Oh, you mean pinball and an ice-cream cone?"

"Something like that," Winston admitted.

"I left my purse at Pedro's," Wendy said.

"I'll treat. It's the least I can do for the girl who threw herself between me and the angry mob back at the house. Have I thanked you in the last five minutes for saving my life? You know I'd do the same for you," Winston added seriously.

"You already have." She gave him a little hug. Carlos rubbed up against her, barking territorially, and suddenly her doubts about Pedro's affection fled. She was the girl with smoke-colored eyes, the only girl for Pedro.

Nina sat on the wrought-iron park bench just

outside Chez Albert. Paul was ten minutes late, and her stomach was growling. Although she hadn't been able to resist a forkful of Winston's legendary pasta, it could hardly satisfy her in the face of the delicious, butter-scented air wafting out of the restaurant.

The worst part about waiting, however, was that it gave her too much time to think about what she was doing there. She'd repeatedly told Paul that she had a boyfriend, but didn't actions speak louder than words? Two nights ago it had been dinner at the elegant Blue Moon Café. "Eating isn't cheating," Paul liked to say with a laugh, and of course he was right. Still—

"Nina!" Winston called as he and Wendy came into view.

Nina waved. "What's up, guys?"

"Murder and mayhem," Winston said cheerfully.

Wendy elbowed him in the ribs. "Hey, don't make fun. Just because it wasn't *your* wallet."

"Sorry," he said contritely, putting an arm around her shoulders and giving her a little hug.

Nina felt as though she was watching act two of a play without having seen act one. "Want to clue me in, guys?"

"We were out walking Carlos, and when we got back to Pedro's condo, someone had broken in and taken my wallet."

"Oh no!" Nina cried.

Wendy's lips quivered. "It's not like life and

death, but I had most of last month's pay in my wallet. Oh, why was I so lazy about getting to the bank? Well, at least they don't seem to have taken anything of Pedro's," she said with a little sigh. "Just smashed his kitchen window, went through my purse, and ran."

"Oh, Wendy, you must be so upset," Nina said. "Did you call the police?"

"Captain Feehan was great," Winston said. "He came right over. He said it's the fourth incident like this in a month. The thief only seems to want cash. The police are on the lookout for someone who's suddenly spending big."

"We better get going," Wendy said. "I want that window fixed tonight. Captain Feehan told us that the bartender at the Beach Bum is the best carpenter around, so I'm going to try to charm him into doing the job."

As her friends headed off toward the boardwalk Nina looked at her watch. Paul was now twenty minutes late. Bored, she began to read the menu posted in one of the lace-curtained windows of Chez Albert.

Escargots in truffle butter . . . a salad of baby greens in a vinaigrette of walnut oil and champagne vinegar . . . lobster, steamed or charcoal grilled, priced according to the market.

Pretty terrific sounding. And pretty expensive. How could Paul afford two extravagant restaurants in one week, anyway? Not on a lifeguard's pay, that was for sure.

All the old suspicions about Paul suddenly came rushing back. The No Swimming sign that had been cut down by someone with a sharp knife—a knife like the one Paul carried when he went diving. The poisoned hot dogs that someone had fed to Paloma Perro. Nothing you could indict a guy for, but he didn't quite add up to Mr. Right either.

Was it possible—an awful thought, but she couldn't keep it from leaping to her mind—was it possible that Paul was the thief?

Chapter Four

Elizabeth almost drove onto the sidewalk when she spotted the titles on the marquee of the Tilton Cineplex. One of the movies playing at the revival house was *Unfinished Business*. The other was *Summer Madness*.

She could scarcely believe how perfectly the titles reflected her feelings. It was almost as if someone had known she was coming.

Could she wind up her unfinished business with Ryan—and not go over the edge? That was the big question. As the slow-moving traffic on busy Main Street ground to a halt, she glanced into the mirror and saw eyes that were huge with doubt. She licked lips that were dry under their coating of raspberry gloss.

Go back before it's too late, an inner voice urged her. But it was already too late. The madness had begun the first time she'd kissed Ryan.

Traffic started moving again. A dark red mini-van pulled out of a space, opening up a choice parking spot. A little thrill ran through her. That clinched it. She was meant to stay.

Get a grip, Wakefield, she murmured. *You're the sensible twin.*

The Trail's End Pub was on the other side of the street, and for a few minutes she just stood there, staring at the green-and-white awning, alternately transfixed with terror and giddily elated at Ryan's nearness. Striving to appear nonchalant, she studied the facade of the restaurant. It looked like a nice enough place, with its wooden shutters and window boxes full of geraniums. The crowd was a pleasant mix of college-age kids and grown-ups.

She knew she'd fit right in. Then again, when Ryan saw her, she'd be as conspicuous as a Christmas tree in August.

"Waiting for someone?"

She whirled around. The guy standing there smiled at her and looked so amazingly much like Tom Watts that she almost shrieked. He was even carrying a copy of an ecology magazine that Tom subscribed to. But it wasn't Tom. He was tucked far away in the mountains of Colorado.

"No, I'm afraid that I'm keeping someone waiting for me," she answered. She offered a brief, cool smile and headed quickly across the street.

She wanted to see Ryan before he saw her, and she pressed herself into the shadows next to one of the windows. Her neck and shoulders tense, she slowly maneuvered until she had perfect sight lines.

She saw a tall, bald waiter with a paunch and a medium-size waiter with lots of curly red hair. Never mind the movie titles on the marquee or the amazing parking space. She'd come to Tilton in vain, she was sure of it. Ryan would be off tonight, or he wouldn't be the Ryan she remembered, or—

Oh. *Oh.*

She was aware that suddenly he was mere inches away from her, even though she was still outside. Nothing separated them but a thin pane of glass.

In his white polo shirt and khakis, Ryan was every bit as handsome as the picture she'd been carrying around in her mind. And yet as she'd feared, he *was* different.

The neat clothes seemed to imprison his strong, athletic body. He'd been designed to work in swim shorts—with nothing else except a sheen of oil and sand on his chest. The forced obliging smile was even worse than the knife-pressed khakis. His expression was meant to radiate authority, command respect. How *dare* the couple he was serving expect him to fetch for them?

Abruptly he lifted his head and gazed toward the street. As their eyes met, Elizabeth felt as though lightning had pierced her soul. She knew that as long as she lived, she would remember the heat of this moment.

"Elizabeth!" he mouthed. "Elizabeth!"

"Ryan," she uttered, and went in.

"Nina, I'm so sorry I'm late," Paul apologized. He took her hand and briefly kissed it—a gesture that no one else Nina knew could have made without looking ridiculous.

Totally together-looking in his pale green linen shirt, pleated white slacks, and deep green summer blazer, he could easily have been a model for an expensive cologne or a fast car. Although he was the one apologizing, Nina felt almost guilty. He'd obviously spent most of those minutes getting slicked up for her, thinking sweet thoughts about her. Meanwhile she'd been busily suspecting him of theft!

The maitre d' offered them a choice, a table in the garden or a corner table in the front room.

"Inside, if you don't mind," Nina said to Paul.

"As long as I'm with you, the scenery's perfect," Paul said. "But if you're worried about getting cold outside, I can always lend you my jacket."

"Actually it's probably cooler inside, with the air conditioning and all," Nina said. She didn't tell him the truth—that the garden sounded too romantic. Inside, she could pretend they were friends having dinner together; outside, there was no denying that they were on a date.

She couldn't help noticing how Paul's attitude about tables contrasted with Bryan's. Her boyfriend believed that African American couples nearly always got inferior seats in restaurants. If he were here with her now, he'd be convinced that the white maitre d' was stowing them out of sight at this corner table. Paul seemed all too pleased that he and Nina were slightly secluded. He immediately ordered a large bottle of Italian mineral water from a hovering waiter.

"I guess the maitre d' can tell we have things to say to each other that shouldn't be overheard," he said. He laughed at Nina's discomfiture. "Although you might want to show this off," he added, putting a beribboned white box on the table.

"For me?" she said foolishly.

"Come on, Nina, open it." Paul's almond-shaped eyes glowed. "It won't bite."

Nina hesitantly opened the box and separated the layers of tissue. Inside, she found the prettiest bracelet she had ever seen—twisted strands of gold, with a sparkling green stone that just happened to match her silk sundress.

"Don't worry," Paul said with a grin. "That's not an emerald. It's just costume jewelry. I'm saving the real stuff for your birthday."

"I can't accept jewelry from you," Nina protested.

"Sure you can. No hidden price tag attached, I promise."

"Paul, I have to tell you, I'm just plain nervous about the way you're spending money on me. I'm

58

not a math major, but I know what lifeguards get paid, and—well, how can you possibly afford to be so extravagant?"

"Relax," he urged her with his ready laugh. "I'm an American. I do it with plastic."

"But charge cards just postpone the problem," Nina said, borrowing a line that Bryan had more than once used on her.

"Aren't you forgetting something? I'm about to be in the money." Paul patted the pocket where he kept his wallet. "The triathlon, baby. No disrespect to those gorgeous legs of yours, but South Beach is going to dust Sweet Valley."

Nina sat up straight. "Forget it. We're going to *vacuum* you."

"It's not even a contest," Paul boasted. "But don't worry, I'm going to spend all your money on you."

Their waiter materialized with the bottle of mineral water that Paul had ordered. "Our special catch of the day—" he began to recite, but Paul cut him off with a wave.

"The special catch of the day is the lady sitting opposite me," he announced, his irresistible smile disarming Nina. "And she'll dine on nothing less than lobster. We'll both have lobster. Do you want yours steamed or grilled?" he asked, directing his attention to Nina.

"I want South Beach skewered, is what I want," she declared. But then again, the lobster sounded wonderful. It had been her favorite food since early on in her privileged childhood. She changed her mind and ordered hers grilled, then she let Paul wind the golden bracelet around her wrist.

A part of her felt that she deserved to be treated this lavishly, but a bigger part knew that her conscience was going to have a hard time digesting the expensive meal and the extravagant gift. She couldn't afford to reciprocate, and she wouldn't really have wanted to do so even if she could have.

What she really wanted, she knew she couldn't have—one guy, with Bryan's principles and Paul's style.

"Hey, relax," Paul said from the other side of the table. "Being good to Nina Harper is a present I'm giving myself. So just resign yourself to having fun, OK?" He pushed a silver butter dish across the table toward her. "Did you notice? They cut the butter to look like little fish. For no other reason than to make us smile. That's what it's all about here. Look around," he said gently.

Nina drank in the atmosphere—the fine oil paintings of seascapes, the lilting notes of a Beethoven string quartet, the beautiful women dressed in silk and their amused-looking escorts. A lot of people had gone to a lot of effort to set the scene, and it would be a shame to waste their good work.

She smiled and relaxed into the beauty of the night.

* * *

While Wendy went off to the Beach Bum, Winston headed for Harry's. Captain Feehan had asked him to put out the word to all local merchants that he was interested in anyone whose spending patterns suddenly changed.

"Are you kidding? Here? I should be so lucky." Harry pointed to a table full of giggling high-school girls. "Maybe it was Sarah Bennett. She ordered bacon on her burger, very suspicious. In fact—" Harry leaned across the counter, rubbing his fingers. "I'd like you to go out on the boardwalk and drum up some sudden spenders. Action on the triathlon, you know?"

"Please, Harry." Winston groaned. "You don't know how much trouble I got into by opening my big mouth on that subject. If Wendy hadn't persuaded everyone that it was the ultimate act of faith on my part—"

"Forget it, no sweat. You're going to be a hero," Harry said. "They'll probably want to name a street after you, they'll be so grateful when it's all over. No, not a street. A street won't be enough." He paused dramatically, then gestured toward the ocean. "They're going to want to rename it the Egbert Ocean."

"Calm down, Har."

"Seriously, this is our big chance." Harry made change for a customer without taking his eyes off Winston. "When you're out and about, just discreetly ask people if they want to place a little wager with Harry and Company. You can be the company, OK? We'll split fifty-fifty."

"Wouldn't that make us bookies?" Winston asked.

Harry's shoulders rose in an eloquent shrug. Who, us? those shoulders seemed to ask. Harry's eyelids fluttered, the picture of milk-and-cookies purity. "That's a gross distortion of an innocently illicit pleasure," he declared in a pained voice. "Try to be a little more sophisticated."

Sophisticated made Winston think of Denise, and thinking of Denise made Winston hungry for money. Not that she was hung up on expensive things, but she was such a good enjoyer that he loved giving her presents.

And he could stand to sophisticate his wardrobe a little. Not that Denise cared about dressing up—she loved browsing thrift shops, the way he did, for great deals—but she did look at him differently on the rare occasion when he wore a coat and tie.

"Consider me sophisticated," he announced to Harry.

"Seal the deal with fries?" Harry asked.

"You bet," Winston said as he reached for the ketchup.

Ryan just stood there as Elizabeth walked through the doorway into the Trail's End Pub.

A cheerful clatter rose and fell around them, but the laughter and clinking of silverware receded into the distance as Elizabeth focused on just one person.

Not a sound came from Ryan. No smile warmed his face.

The romantic tension between them had somehow turned into just plain tension the minute she'd crossed the threshold.

"Well, hi," she finally said, with an artificial brightness that twanged in her own ears.

"Hi," he returned. The syllable seemed to require effort. He blinked rapidly, as if his contact lenses were suddenly bothering him.

"You're looking well," she said.

"You too," he returned. "How's the gang?" he asked stiffly. He looked down at his strong hands when he spoke.

"Everyone's OK," she said. She drew a deep breath. "I want to talk with you, Ryan. I mean *talk*."

"Well, sure, Elizabeth. Sure," he said wearily. "But I've got to finish my shift." He glanced at his watch. "I've got an hour to go. Want to come back?"

"No," she said quickly. She knew that if she left, she would get into the Jeep and drive home. Or she would come back on time only to find that he had once again vanished to an unknown destination.

Ryan glanced around the crowded room. "Looks like all the tables are taken."

His voice sounded robotic. She wanted to shake him.

63

"I'll wait at the bar," she said firmly.

A guy stood up and dropped a dollar next to his beer mug. She moved quickly to claim the vacant stool. Ryan came up behind her then, and for a moment she could have sworn she smelled salt water and tanning oil.

"Arthur, this is my friend Elizabeth," he said to the bartender. "Take care of her, will you?"

"My pleasure," Arthur said. He was a handsome heavyset man with wavy hair. "What'll it be, Elizabeth?"

"A ginger ale, please," she said.

He spritzed soda into a pint mug. "Looks like great weather for Labor Day, huh?"

"Yeah, great," she echoed with all the enthusiasm she could muster. But as she watched Ryan clear a table and speed back toward the kitchen, she felt as if chilly winds were blowing and storm clouds were gathering.

The moonlit surf was like a drum pounding out the beat as Jessica and Ben ran side by side along the empty beach.

They were both dressed in black—a T-shirt and spandex tights for Jessica, a T-shirt and sweats for Ben—and both were barefoot. Jessica loved the way they blended in with the shadows or were splattered with moonlight, depending on what the swiftly moving clouds were doing.

"Open up your stride, Jess," Ben urged her. "No, don't tense your jaw; that saps your energy.

Let the running happen through you. Yes. Beautiful. Yes."

She couldn't ever remember feeling stronger or happier. Listening to the wind whistle past her ears, she seemed to be lifted out of gravity's pull, blown along like a grain of sand.

Loving Ben was like that too—demanding yet oddly effortless, and good for both body and soul. How wonderfully different he was from the other guys she'd loved!

And how different she was from the Jessica who had loved those other guys. As she raced through the night, images from her past bombarded her. She saw the confused, rebellious child-woman who'd let herself get swept up into a marriage with Mike McAllery—a union as bitter as it was brief. And then there was the desperate, ditzy Jessica who'd jumped into shark-infested waters to attract the best-looking guy on a cruise ship, Randy Mason.

Hot-tempered, fast-driving Mike had turned out to be a womanizer. The *idea* of Randy had been romantic—the former nerd who'd transformed himself into her mysterious guardian angel—but the reality had been disappointing. One way or another, they'd all disappointed her. The trouble was, she couldn't stand being unattached. So she'd leaped first and taken a close look second—again and again.

And this summer had threatened to produce another typical scenario. She'd convinced herself that

Ryan was the guy for her, and she'd just about thrown herself at him, demanding love he didn't want to give her and spurning the love that Ben was clearly offering.

And now she seemed to have a future as well as a wonderful present. But the past was still behind her, like a competitor breathing down her neck, spurring her to run at a speed she'd thought unattainable.

Faster, faster, Jess. Leave your old life behind you.

"You were amazing!" Ben shouted as she finally fell to the sand in an exhausted heap. "What did it? What made you take off like that?"

She panted in his arms, loving the feel and the smell of their mingled sweat. "I was trying to outrun my past," she mumbled. "I think I wanted to put the whole world between me and every guy who wasn't you."

He kissed her softly, his blue eyes gleaming with tender understanding. "Don't feel haunted by your past, Jess. I'm not."

His words were like a beautiful rose. She could almost feel the soft, dewy petals unfolding inside her heart. She wanted to believe she deserved it, but something in her still doubted it. "Really?" she said. "You swear?"

"Really," Ben assured her, stroking her hair.

"You won't forget all about me when you go back to Chicago?" She shivered and thought of all those miles between them.

"You'll still be my girl," he declared. "And I

know I'll still be your guy," he added.

The smell of salt air tickled Jessica's nose. She heard the rustle of some low-flying night creature above them. Suddenly she was so full of good feeling, there was no room for doubt. If only this summer could last forever!

Well, maybe they could make it summer all year round.

"Ben, couldn't you transfer to SVU?" she pleaded. "It's not all basket weaving and gym classes."

"I know," he said. "But it's not the school for me any more than U of C is the school for you. I intend to rack up those frequent-flier miles, though. I'm going to come see you so often, every airline in America is going to want to fly that route."

"If we win the race—and the bet," Jessica said.

"There's no *if* about it," Ben declared. "Not if you run the way you did tonight. Will you? For us?"

"I will," Jessica promised fervently.

Wendy loved strolling the boardwalk with Carlos. Paloma Perro might be the original huggable mutt, but Carlos had his own terrific doggy dignity. Thanks to his expensive groomer, he was very sleek and had a musky smell—a gentleman among canines.

Everyone smiled at Carlos, and Carlos wagged his caramel-colored tail at everyone. Even members of the South Beach Lifeguard Squad loved him.

Even the most obnoxious members of that squad, Rachel Max and Tina Fong, who were just then looming up out of the evening crowd a hundred yards from Harry's.

As the two girls bent to pat Carlos, Wendy shriveled inside. Rachel looked Hollywood glamorous tonight, her height accentuated by strappy high-heeled sandals and her curves and gleaming tan set off by a gauzy white dress with a missing midriff. Petite Tina's jet black hair had been freshly cut, and its crisp planes swung alluringly over cheeks whose tawny color and perfect roundness she'd played up with plum-color blush.

Why couldn't I have gotten a smidgen less wit and character in exchange for, oh, even just long, thick eyelashes? Wendy moaned to herself for about the millionth time.

"Dog walks dog," Wendy heard Tina mutter under her breath, followed by a giggle.

That was so mean, even by South Beach standards, that Wendy had a hard time believing her own ears. But judging from the smirk on Rachel's face, Wendy had heard right.

"Careful, Tina," Wendy said in a sickeningly sweet voice. "Carlos likes to have dinner promptly at seven, and I haven't fed him yet. But then again, I promised my boyfriend that I wouldn't let Carlos eat anything tough."

"Boyfriend?" Rachel threw back the word as if it were a skinny little fish that had somehow had the nerve to take her hook.

Wendy's stomach churned. Why, oh why, had she let these awful girls trick her into playing their put-down game? But she had, and now she had to beat them at it.

"Boyfriend," she enunciated overcarefully. "Though really it would be more accurate to call him my man friend. Pedro Paloma isn't just some college kid."

Rachel and Wendy exchanged a glance and shared a sneer.

"Did you spend too much time in the sun today, dear?" Rachel asked.

"Yes, you better take two aspirin and lie down," Tina chimed in.

"We're not being nice, Tina," Rachel said in mock repentance. "Her fantasy romance is probably the only kind she'll ever have—let's leave it alone."

Wendy gestured with Carlos's leash. "If I'm not his girlfriend, then why do I walk his dog every evening?" she asked with all the haughtiness she could muster.

"For the same reason your friend Winston waddles around in a hamburger roll," Tina said. "You're getting paid to do it. You're a caretaker." She made the word sound practically criminal.

"I am not!" Wendy fumed. "I walk Pedro because I love Carlos and he loves me!"

As the two other girls burst into peals of hilarity, she realized her mistake.

"I mean *Pedro* loves me!" Wendy all but shouted.

Too late. The damage was done. Rachel and Tina were walking away, their arms around each other's shoulders and their beautiful heads thrown back in derisive laughter that sounded as though it would echo until the end of time.

Wendy stood rooted to the spot, her gray eyes filling with tears. Winston would tell her that she was wonderful and these girls were awful, but that wouldn't make it right—nothing would make it right.

Yes, something would. Beating those horrible girls and their friends in the triathlon would make things *very* right.

We're going to win, she vowed with a competitive ferocity she'd never before felt. *We're going to smoosh them into smithereens.*

No matter what we have to do, we're going to win.

Arthur the bartender gestured at Elizabeth's empty glass of ginger ale. "Another round?"

"No, thanks," she said disconsolately. If she drank any more of the stuff, she was going to float away. She'd been sitting there for over an hour.

The bartender applied his rag to the surface in front of Elizabeth. "Think the weather'll hold for Labor Day weekend?" he asked.

She shook her head in disbelief. This had to be the fourth time he'd brought up the Labor Day weekend weather as if it were some new and terrifically exciting scientific breakthrough.

70

"Summer flew by, didn't it? Hard to believe it's almost over." He picked up Elizabeth's glass, tossed out the half-melted ice, squirted soda into it, and put it back down in front of her. "On the house. Though to tell you the truth, it looks as if you need more than ginger ale to fix what's ailing you." Chortling at his own wit, he ambled off to deal with an impatient knot of beer guzzlers at the far end of the bar.

In despair Elizabeth made a vow. If Ryan didn't come back within five minutes, she would leave. The restaurant was packed, and she didn't doubt that he was having trouble getting free, but she'd needed a lot of nerve to come here tonight and it was his turn to make an effort.

As though he'd read the message in her stiffening shoulders, she saw Ryan suddenly set down a tray of dirty glasses on a service station and head toward her. "Elizabeth," he began. "I'm—" Then his gaze shifted to the doorway. "Oh no," he muttered.

Elizabeth stared mutely as a pretty red-haired girl made a beeline for Ryan and put a proprietary hand on his arm. "I'm sorry I wasn't there when you called before. Everything OK?" Ryan nodded, and the girl looked relieved. "Then I'll meet you as soon as you get off," the girl said. "The usual place."

As she turned and left, Ryan offered Elizabeth a sickly smile.

"You probably wonder—" he began lamely.

Elizabeth thought that she'd rather die than hear whatever story he was busily concocting.

"Please, Ryan," she said, biting back rage and pain. "No need to explain anything. I just came because everyone wanted to make sure you were all right, and clearly you are."

And I'm not even slightly all right, but I'm going to get out of here before you see that.

She swung her bag over her shoulder and started to walk out, praying that she'd make it to her car before the tears poured down her cheeks. Suddenly she felt a hand grip her arm.

"Elizabeth, wait!"

The strength in his grasp and the intensity in his voice belonged to the Ryan she once knew, the Ryan she maybe loved. Lips aching for a kiss, ears ready for healing words, she turned to face him.

"Elizabeth," he said again, seeming to savor the taste of her name. But suddenly he shrank away. His eyes clouded over as if in fear.

"I just wanted to say that it was, um, nice to see you," he said limply.

Elizabeth thought she might roar in frustration. "Ryan!" she cried. "Can't we talk? Really talk?"

"No," he said through tight lips. "We can't. At least I can't."

She stumbled out of there, propelled herself toward the car, and flung herself into the driver's seat with a single sob of frustration.

"That's it!" she cried out into the night as she

headed toward the highway. "My unfinished business is finished! Good-bye, Ryan Taylor!"

As Nina and Paul walked across the beach toward her house, the sea breeze suddenly picked up and she shivered violently. Paul whipped off his sport coat and put it around her shoulders.

The green linen jacket might have been a magician's cape, it made her feel so transformed. Paul's body heat seemed to swirl around her. She could almost taste the citrus spice of his cologne.

Under his spell, she was powerless as his arms wrapped around her waist. "Paul, Paul," she murmured as his lips came down on hers.

The sea and the wind seemed to echo his name. *Paul. Paul. Paul.*

His kisses became more demanding. Her lips felt as though they might melt beneath the heat and the pressure of his mouth. Her lips parted, and she felt as though they were breathing a single breath.

The warmth spread, suffusing her entire body, making every inch of her feel kissed. Her shoulders tingled. Her fingers. Her toes.

His hands moved possessively over her—a little too possessively. As if an invisible line had been crossed, Nina snapped to her senses. The instant she resisted, Paul pulled back without protest, taking her hand lightly in his and continuing toward the house.

He was so easygoing now, she was almost

miffed. Of course she wanted him to respect her wishes—but was it really her wishes she had acted on? Or was it her sense of what her wishes *ought* to be?

But really, there was no choice. She was committed to Bryan. Period and end of sentence.

"Paul—" she began, but in a different tone of voice—the voice of reason.

"I know," he said calmly. "You've got a boyfriend."

"Yup."

"I just hope he knows how lucky he is," Paul declared.

"He does," Nina said loyally.

But she knew that the confidence in her voice was hiding her own inner doubts.

Sure, Bryan knew he was lucky, but at the same time he sort of took her for granted. He didn't put a whole lot of effort into their relationship. Maybe that was why his kisses didn't tingle and provoke her the way Paul's did.

And the worst part was, she didn't know whether that meant she should go on kissing Paul or never again trust herself to be alone with him.

Wendy fretfully turned her pillow over, looking for a cool spot to lay her cheek against. Her cotton blanket kept bunching up. She kicked it off and then pulled it around her again. And still her body felt edgy and just plain wrong, as if she were coming down with the flu. She wanted ice water.

She wanted hot tea. She wanted her mother. She wanted to hide in a mile-deep hole and never again see anyone.

Mostly she wanted tonight not to have happened.

She stared out at the star-spangled sky and moon-splashed sea and tried to focus on the big picture. But all she could think of was Rachel and Tina's hoots of laughter and their horribly cruel words.

Dog walks dog. Caretaker.

For the first time in years, she hated her own face. Wild thoughts raced through her mind. She would perm her unpermable hair, spend every penny of her summer pay on a makeover, throw herself at the feet of some plastic surgeon and beg for a little nothing nose, a heart-shaped chin. Then, when she was a famous model, she'd make Rachel and Tina writhe with envy. . . .

Suddenly Pedro's face seemed to loom in front of her. "But they're already writhing, my sweet, silly Wendy. Don't you see? They're green with jealousy. As green as the sea. Because Pedro Paloma loves you."

"Go away." She swatted the air. "I have enough problems. I don't need an imaginary lover. That's all you are, isn't it? How come you haven't called in four days?"

"I call you every night when I sing—you just don't know how to hear me. Shall I sing to you now?"

"Pedro," she mumbled sleepily, "is this a dream?"

"Yes, sweet Wendy. But everything you're dreaming is true. Listen to me now."

A C-major chord rang from his guitar. She clutched her pillows as his voice filled her head:

> *The girl with smoke-colored eyes*
> *Has set my soul on fire*
> *The girl with smoke-colored eyes*
> *Makes me feel I won life's prize*
> *She's everything I desire*
>
> *She came up from the waters*
> *She came down from the skies*
> *Her laughter sounds like summer*
> *I cannot live without her*
> *The girl with smoke-colored eyes*
>
> *Go to sleep, my darling*
> *Enough of tears and sighs*
> *My loving thoughts surround you*
> *My arms entwine around you*
> *Close your smoke-colored eyes*
> *Oh, close your smoke-colored eyes.*

*Chapter
Five*

_____

Nina looked at Elizabeth across their cereal bowls
and didn't like what she saw. Elizabeth looked
wiped out—and not just with physical exhaustion.
She looked as if the famous Elizabeth Wakefield
spirit were running on empty.

"Did you sleep last night, Liz? Your eyes are really red."

"That's funny," Elizabeth said. "I was about to
tell you the same thing. Oh, well. At least we
match our official red swimsuits." She pushed
away her half-eaten cereal.

Nina sternly shook her head. "Don't even
think about going out there without finishing
breakfast. Every last little crunchy morsel in the
bowl and all the raisins too. And drink your or-
ange juice. You'll need your strength out there
today."

"Yes, Mom. So why do *you* look so terrible? I

heard you come in last night. It wasn't all that late."

"Yeah, but getting in is one thing and falling asleep is another," Nina rejoined. She spooned Winston's mango preserves onto her English muffin.

"Did Paul give you a rough time?" Elizabeth asked.

"No, darn it, he gave me a good time. Too good a time," Nina answered with a glum laugh. "So what's your excuse?"

"Nothing special," Elizabeth said evasively.

"Oh, thanks a lot." Nina got up and carried her dishes and juice glass over to the dishwasher. "How come you always pry my secrets out of me and then clam up about yours?"

As she opened the dishwasher she noticed that someone—Jessica, no doubt—had put in a wood-handled knife that was supposed to be washed by hand. *Honestly!* Did she have to be in charge of absolutely everything, even the care and feeding of Mrs. Krebbs's kitchen implements?

"What secret? I didn't hear any secrets," Elizabeth said. "Every time you go out with Paul, you have fun. And every time you have fun, you feel guilty about Bryan. That's old news."

"Well, it was a little different last night," Nina said. Grabbing the knife, she rinsed it under the faucet.

"He kissed me," she went on. Her back was to Elizabeth, which made it easier to say the words.

"And I kissed him back. And I really enjoyed it. Satisfied?" She wiped the knife dry on a dish towel. "Now tell me what *you* did last night."

"Last night," Elizabeth began, biting her lip. "Last night I *didn't* get kissed. Satisfied?"

"No, and apparently neither are you," Nina retorted, turning around. She drew an exasperated breath, then softened at the stricken look on Elizabeth's face. "It's OK, Liz. You don't have to tell me."

But as they grabbed their gear and headed for the lifeguard station, Nina wondered if she was doing Elizabeth any favors by letting her off the hook so easily. Elizabeth's shoulders sagged, and her head was down. She looked as though she might burst from feelings held in check too long.

Not that Nina had confided all her own feelings. How her heart had beaten so fast as Paul's lips had pressed against hers that she'd thought she might faint. How that same heart had lurched with guilt when she'd gotten back to her room and looked at Bryan's picture on her bedside table.

She suddenly found herself longing for summer to be over. Once she was back on campus, life would straighten itself out again.

She pictured herself and Bryan sitting in one of their usual haunts, like the unpretentious diner he favored.

She visualized his intense dark face as he'd lean across the Formica table in the diner. Then he'd kiss her—almost as passionately as Paul had last night.

"Nina!"

Jessica's voice burst through the fantasy. Nina looked up. She and Elizabeth had arrived at the lifeguard station, and the whole crew was there—and something seemed very much to be the matter.

Her heart started to pound. The beach wasn't open for swimming yet, but had someone gone into the water anyway? Had someone gotten into trouble?

"What's up?" she demanded crisply.

"Someone broke into the station last night," tall, redheaded Kerry Janowitz explained.

"And busted open the locked drawer!" Jessica chimed in.

"Five bucks on Sweet Valley."

"A ten spot says South Shore."

"Hey, Winston, you giving odds?"

"My money's on Sweet Valley . . . and can I get a little action on the Yankee–Red Sox game tonight too?"

"Whoa, there. One at a time," Winston cried, scribbling in the notebook he kept tucked in a pocket beneath his hamburger costume.

He could hardly believe how much interest there was in the triathlon. Some of these people looked as though they hadn't even had breakfast yet, and here they were eagerly placing bets on the competition. As he made his morning tour of the sunny beach he was actually attracting more attention than the gray-haired man and woman who were stilt walking along the tide line.

If wagering weren't such an, um, innocently sophisticated pastime, he would be tempted to think that this group of bettors was a little sick. As in, compulsive. His friends might all be great athletes, but the triathlon wasn't exactly the Olympics.

Come to think of it, several of the people pressing five-dollar bills into his hand looked less than wholesome. Pasty skinned and stoop shouldered in the bright light, as though they'd been hunched over a card table all night. The kind of people who made you want to mutter, "Get a life."

"No action on baseball," Winston said sternly to the badly shaven man who had inquired. "That would be . . . *gambling*."

As he uttered the last word, his ringing sincerity moved him. Really, taking bets on the triathlon was totally different from taking other kinds of bets. It was drumming up interest in a great cause—sort of like selling Girl Scout cookies.

"You like shortbread, I like mint," he sang nonsensically as he ambled along. "You like summer, I like wint. . . ."

Nina stared grimly at the top drawer of the built-in wood desk. A two-inch-wide hole, where the lock cylinder had been, made it look as though someone had wanted to inflict damage, not just steal. She shivered in her red swimsuit.

The others clustered around her—Wendy, Ben, Elizabeth, Jessica, and the three lifeguards who didn't live in the house: Kerry Janowitz, willowy Paula McFee, and the guy who Paula said had taught her that short is beautiful, Marcus Collier.

"Look at how they took the brass thingie right out of it," Jessica said.

"I don't believe it," Wendy exclaimed. "First Pedro's window and now this."

"Was anything in the drawer?" Ben asked practically.

"Nope." Kerry shook his red head. "I was the last one to leave, and when I took out my stuff, I remember thinking that it felt sort of dopey to lock an empty drawer."

"Yeah, well, Ryan really drilled it into us that you always lock the drawer," Paula said.

A silence filled the air at the mention of Ryan's name. Nina could feel Elizabeth stiffen next to her.

"Who could have done this?" Marcus asked. He ran a hand through his blond crewcut. "I mean, it's not as if we kept lots of money or jewelry in there. Was it really a thief or just someone who wanted to bug us? You know, make us jittery."

"Well, if they wanted us to be jumpy, they succeeded." Nina hugged herself in a vain effort to warm up. Kerry untied the yellow sweatshirt he wore around his red lifeguard trunks, and

Nina gratefully slipped it over her head.

"Hey, maybe it's some alien invaders," Ben said sarcastically. "Or our sworn enemies from South Beach. Maybe they planted a microphone in there."

"Why?" Elizabeth returned in the same tone of voice. "To overhear you and Jessica whispering sweet nothings to each other?"

"Don't be a jerk," Jessica said, glaring at her sister. "But I bet Rachel and her crew would love to hear us plan our triathlon strategy. Isn't that what you meant, Ben?"

"Exactly." He put his arm around her. "I wouldn't put it past Rachel."

Marcus held up his hand and winked. "I think we should draft Winston for our squad," he said loudly, directing his voice toward the drawer. "He'll be our secret weapon."

"Winston can really move when he wants to," Wendy protested hotly.

"You mean like when there's food on the table?" Marcus returned. "Hey, easy, Wendy, don't hit—I was only joking." Nina frowned as some of the others laughed. "It's no joke," she said. "We have to have eight people and a sub to qualify for the triathlon, and it doesn't look as though Ryan's coming back. Who else is there except Winston?"

"Paloma Perro?" Marcus suggested.

"I still say we should check out the drawer," Ben said. Edging past Nina, he pulled it open and peered inside. "Guess what, guys?" His voice was excited. "I was right! There is a bug." He stuck his hand into the drawer, then solemnly displayed his trophy.

It was a small, gray, long-legged, sleepy-looking spider.

"Of course, technically it's not a bug, it's an arachnid—" Ben began.

"I love spiders!" Wendy said. "Remember *Charlotte's Web*? Let me see it." Plucking the creature from Ben's hand, she suddenly whirled around and dropped it down the back of Marcus's T-shirt.

"You can move too," she declared with a laugh as Marcus squealed and wriggled. "Don't worry, I know my arachnids—it's not poisonous."

Nina's stomach tightened. She was on the verge of panic again, and not because of the spider.

"Chill, everybody," she commanded. "We've got a pair of serious problems here. One is security, and the other is the triathlon. If we don't stop horsing around, we're going to go home with about two cents between us."

"Maybe we need to take turns guarding the lifeguard station," Marcus said. He laughed at his own wit, then clapped a hand over his mouth. "Sorry, I didn't mean to be funny."

"It *wasn't* funny," Nina snapped.

But it wasn't really Marcus who'd upset her. Her thoughts kept drifting to Paul.

He could easily have dropped by the lifeguard station after walking her back to the beach house last night.

He'd been awfully interested in the empty beach house, hadn't he? Empty—and with a lock he'd boasted he could pick.

And she'd wondered how he could afford the fancy dinner and the jewelry. Was he involved in shady dealings of some kind?

You're being paranoid, she chided herself.

But maybe he'd been ticked off that she'd refused to set another date with him. Would he have taken his anger out on the lifeguard station?

No matter which way she looked at it, Paul was her number-one suspect.

Walking back into the house after the squad meeting, Elizabeth heard the telephone ring.

"Long distance calling Ms. Elizabeth Wakefield—"

Elizabeth had the sinking feeling that her mother was on the line. She'd sent her parents and her brother, Steven, some cute postcards, but she hadn't called home since July Fourth. There was too much she didn't feel like talking about.

She adjusted her voice to Jessica's slightly higher pitch. "Elizabeth's not here right now. Can I take a message?" The real Elizabeth would have said, grammatically, "May I take a message?"

She heard the operator ask whether the person at the other end wanted to have the call returned. "That's all right," Elizabeth heard, and her heart leaped. *Tom!*

"Operator, hold on," she said eagerly. "Here comes Elizabeth now. Yoo-hoo, Elizabeth," she sang out. "Phone call. Person-to-person." Glad that no one else was in the house to witness her silliness, she then spoke into the phone using her own, slightly lower voice. "Hello. This is Elizabeth Wakefield."

"Liz, was that you all along?" Tom asked. She could almost hear his grin.

"Guilty as charged." Clutching the phone, she tumbled backward onto the living-room couch. Suddenly she felt really good inside. It was delicious to be known as well as Tom knew her—Tom and nobody else.

"Avoiding bill collectors?" he teased. "That's more the other Ms. Wakefield's style."

"Well, this is the summer Jess and I switched styles," Elizabeth returned, suddenly serious.

"You mean you're walking around in Jessica's cutoffs?" Tom's words were light, but Elizabeth thought she could hear a note of anxiety.

"I wasn't talking about clothes, but it's not really a conversation for the phone," she said. "We can talk about it when we're back together," she added, saying the words with a ringing emphasis that was meant to reassure herself as well as him.

"You didn't swap me as part of the bargain, did you?" Tom's bantering tone didn't quite cover his own seriousness. "Because I was calling to tell you that I miss you. You, Elizabeth."

"I miss you too," she said. "I'm wearing the T-shirt you sent me."

"Really? I bet the Rocky Mountains never

looked better. Um, wait, I'm not sure that came out the way I meant it to."

She laughed. It felt as though she hadn't really laughed in ages.

"I thought you were supposed to be improving your communications skills this summer," she teased.

"All we did today was listen to someone drone on about FCC regulations," Tom lamented. "If you ask me, we need to regulate our legislators more and our broadcasting stations less."

"I couldn't agree more," Elizabeth said. She huddled against the couch cushions, searching for the sweet warmth she'd be feeling if Tom were there in person. "Then again, I guess the regulations prove how much power you have when your voice goes out over the airwaves. Aren't you glad the people in Washington are afraid of you?"

They talked for a while, moving easily from issues to jokes to their own special brand of tenderness the way they always did. Finally Tom said with obvious reluctance, "I've got a class. I better hang up."

"I'm so glad you called," Elizabeth said sincerely.

"I could stay on all day." Tom's voice was warm. "Even at daytime rates."

"Me too," she said.

"I'll call you again soon."

"Or I'll call you," Elizabeth promised.

"Here's a kiss for your nose. Is it sunburned?"

"No," Elizabeth said. "But it needs a kiss anyway. Here's a kiss for your ear. Is it worn out from all those lectures?"

"Just about ready to fall off, but your kiss saved it," Tom said. "Well, I hate to hang up, but—"

"Me too. Let's do it together," Elizabeth said. "On the count of three. One—"

"One and a half," Tom said.

She laughed. "Two and three-eighths."

"Three," they said together, and hung up.

Afterward Elizabeth lay on the couch, clutching a pillow. She and Tom could talk for a hundred years and not run out of things to say.

Yes, she was very lucky to be loved by Tom Watts. He was one great guy—as committed to her as he was to making the world a better place. And yet—

Ryan.

She squeezed her eyes shut, as if that might somehow banish the unbidden name. But she was unsuccessful. She bolted to her feet, flinging down the pillow.

How *dare* she think about another guy just seconds after telling Tom that she loved and missed him? She flashed back to the terrible hurt she'd experienced when she'd caught Tom kissing his high-school girlfriend, Nicole. They'd run into each other unexpectedly when the Sweet Valley gang had all gone on a spring break cruise. The incident had just about ruined the vacation—and not just for the two of them. All their friends had gotten caught up in a stormy debate over the ethics of the situation.

In a way what she was doing was much worse. The kiss between Tom and Nicole had lasted only a few seconds, and Tom had been sincerely regretful and eager to put it behind him. Her thoughts about Ryan seemed to be an endless spiral that she was in no hurry to escape.

The screech of a gull sounded through the open windows. Walking to the front of the living room, she gazed out at the ocean. A flock of birds was rising in a V formation, brilliant in the afternoon light.

She and Tom were birds of a feather. Everyone seemed to think that the two of them would soar to the heights as long as they flew together.

But were they as alike as they seemed? Or was there a wildness in herself that she was just beginning to know—a wildness that made her want to fly in some different, crazy sky? With that strange bird called Ryan?

Elizabeth watched wave after wave tumble toward the shore in front of the house, bringing seaweed and shells, garbage and treasures, but none brought her an answer.

Winston's latest customer was a little old lady with blue-gray hair. She took two crumpled dollar bills out of an ancient beaded change purse and waved them at him.

"I'm going to bet on South Beach because my

name is Sylvia Barlow, and if you can't believe in your own initials, what can you believe in?"

"Absolutely," Winston said vigorously. "If you can't bet on your own name, nothing is sure in this life."

He noticed Ben Mercer jogging determinedly his way, and he didn't want to be found in the middle of this transaction. He reached for the bills. But the blue-haired lady kept them tightly in her clutch.

"Then again, my name was Sylvia Van Sykes before I married Mr. Barlow, may he rest in peace, so perhaps—"

Winston tucked away his notebook. "Ma'am? If you want to sleep on it—"

She shook her head. "At my age, young man, you don't sleep on anything." Fishing in her purse, she brought out another pair of bills. "I was happy as Sylvia Van Sykes and happy as Sylvia Barlow, so you know what I'm going to do? I'm going to bet two dollars on each team," she declared triumphantly.

As she walked away, a satisfied smile on her face, Winston decided that gambling was a strange subculture. A very strange subculture. An innocent vice, but a truly weird one. If the amounts of money being pressed into his hand weren't so insignificant, he might almost feel peculiar about being a part of it. Almost. But Sylvia Van Sykes Barlow was wearing an expensive-looking loose silk shirt over her white toreador pants, and her big earrings looked like real gold to his eye, so there wasn't the teensiest tinsiest reason to feel peculiar about taking her two dollars—her four dollars. Right?

"Winston!" Ben held out his hand, and for an uneasy moment Winston feared he'd seen the notebook. Then Ben said, "Congrats. You've been elected an honorary member of the Sweet Valley Shore Lifeguard Squad."

"I have?" Winston blinked with pleasure. "No joke?"

"No joke."

Winston flushed with pride and immediately became aware that he was wearing about twenty pounds of hamburger costume. He visualized himself jumping into the water to save some child and instantly going under like a stone.

Oh, maybe that was the point. Maybe his friends had decided that they'd let him off the hook too easily.

"But I repeat, it's honorary," Ben was saying. "Because we want you to know that we love you even though you may have ruined our lives. Just teasing," he added hastily, patting Winston on the lettuce. "Not about loving you, about ruining our lives."

"But I get to participate in the triathlon?" Winston asked. He tried to focus on the uplifting aspects of pulling with his friends, not on the grueling realities.

"You do and you don't," Ben said. "Your

name's on the list so we can have the legal number of participants. But you're just a sub. And frankly, we don't intend to need you."

"Don't call me frankly. I'm a hamburger," Winston tossed off. But he couldn't hold back a wave of sadness.

"Winston, there are a lot of great people in the world who aren't athletes," Ben said kindly. "Admit it—do you really want to bike for ten miles, swim for half a mile in the ocean, then run a mile in full scuba gear except for the flippers?"

"Sure I do," Winston said. "Spread out over the next couple of years," he added with a rueful smile.

"Exactly."

"I'll pray for the continued health of everyone on the squad," Winston solemnly declared.

A part of Elizabeth's mind seemed to slip loose from its moorings and float overhead, detachedly observing the rest of her. *Get a grip,* she heard herself say to herself. *You've been standing at the living-room window for half an hour now. Has the ocean hypnotized you?*

I don't want to get a grip, she dreamily answered herself. *I've always had a grip. I'm tired of being wonderful Elizabeth Wakefield. Let me go.*

A loud rapping at the front door jarred Elizabeth out of her reverie.

She opened the door and saw the familiar figure of Captain Feehan, the police officer in charge of all the local lifesaving teams. He was about the same age as Elizabeth's father and had the same reassuring effect on her.

"Oh, hi," she said. "Don't tell me you already figured out who broke into the lifeguard station!"

"Thanks for the compliment, but not even Dick Tracy would have figured it out that fast. Give me a few hours. I mostly came to drop off these circulars about the triathlon," Captain Feehan said. "Hot off the presses." He handed Elizabeth a stack of green sheets of paper.

"Speaking of hot, want to come in for some lemonade?" Elizabeth asked impulsively.

"I can't drink—I'm on duty," he quipped. "Actually, lemonade sounds super. You kids are sure looking after this house," he commented as he followed her to the kitchen. He took off his straw hat and ran his fingers through his sandy hair. "Some summer folks don't give a hoot— they track in sand, leave wet towels everywhere, you name it. Hey, not to change the subject, but have you seen Paul today?"

"No, I haven't."

"Well, if you do, will you please ask him to drop by the police station?"

Elizabeth was surprised by the request, but she just shrugged. "Sure," she said. "Glad to."

She got a pair of tall glasses down from the cupboard, dropped three ice cubes into each one, and took the lemonade pitcher out of the refrigerator. The glasses and the pitcher had a homey, old-fashioned design on them—slices of lemon and sprigs of mint.

"We were kind of slobby in the beginning," she confessed as she poured. "But when Nina became head lifeguard, she turned into a neatnik. I guess the rest of us found it easier to pick up after ourselves than listen to her scoldings."

"She's done a great job," Captain Feehan said. "You all have." He took a sip, then nodded appreciatively. "This didn't come from a can, I bet."

"Winston made it. He boils the water and the sugar first, then adds the lemon juice."

"Well, it sure hits the spot." Captain Feehan took off his omnipresent sunglasses, wiped them on his shirt, and then put them back on.

The momentary glimpse of his eyes—pale blue and tired looking—emboldened Elizabeth. She leaned across the kitchen table.

"Why did Ryan abandon us?" she asked. "Do you know?"

Captain Feehan's lips tightened. "Last summer a child drowned. Ryan wasn't on duty, but he blamed himself."

"Nina told us about it at the beginning of the summer. To make us all realize how serious our job was. That must have been so horrible." Elizabeth shuddered. "But what does it have to do with this summer?"

"I guess we all blamed ourselves," Captain Feehan went on. "But Ryan took it harder than anyone else. Maybe something happened this summer that brought it all back."

Elizabeth recalled the distracting kiss she and Ryan had shared and his unhappiness because Elizabeth, not he, had been alert enough to break the clinch and save a helpless young surfer. Feeling herself flush scarlet at the complicated and confusing memory, Elizabeth hastily drank from her glass to cover her reaction. Had Ryan's relationship with a girl been somehow connected with the tragic accident of the previous summer?

"I still don't quite understand," she persisted. "Why would he just run away?"

"Look, he's a great guy, he's got a lot going for him, but he—" Abruptly Captain Feehan broke off. "I'm sorry, Elizabeth, I can't solve the mystery. The only person who can do that is Ryan. I know it's hard for you, and I wish I could do more to help."

He stood up and carried his glass to the sink. "Thanks again for the lemonade."

After Captain Feehan left, Elizabeth decided to wash the glasses by hand so their pretty design wouldn't fade in the dishwasher. As she picked one up to suds it, it slipped from her fingers and shattered on the linoleum-covered floor. "Oh no!" she exclaimed. She sadly picked up the largest of the shards. It looked as though one of the lemon slices in the design had been sawed in half.

She got out the broom and dustpan. Tears filled her eyes. She knew she was in danger of shattering something far more precious—her relationship with Tom. But she had to understand the enigma called Ryan.

Well, she might not know much about him, but she was more than ever certain of one thing. He was wounded, and he needed comforting. And she was the one to do it—the one to put her arms around him and hold him and let him shed his tears and his fears.

But what about the girl at the Trail's End Pub? Was that *her* mission too? She'd seemed important to Ryan, but if he cared deeply about her, how could she explain the crackling electricity between him and Elizabeth?

Carlos strained at his leash as they neared Pedro's house. His tail wagged like crazy.

Wendy's heart danced in hopeful excitement. Was Carlos trying to tell her that his master was home? Was it possible that Pedro had returned from his tour while she was out walking the hound? She broke into a run.

As she raced up the front sidewalk Wendy glimpsed movement in the shrubs behind the house, and her excitement changed to fear. The kitchen window! Maybe the burglar had come back for more!

Her mind whirled. If she confronted the intruder, she might be in danger, but if she ran to a neighbor, the intruder might escape.

Holding tight to Carlos's leash, she inched toward the back of the house. She wouldn't confront the guy, she decided, but if she at least got a glimpse of him, she could give his description to the police.

As she rounded the corner a hand reached out and grabbed her wrist. Another hand stifled her scream.

Her eyes widened in terror and then in recognition.

Paul!

As Ben walked away, Winston couldn't help envisioning the headline on the sports page:

Sweet Valley Sub Subdues South Shore in Triathlon Triumph

Winston Egbert brought honor to the word *honorary* today with his heroic last-minute participation in the traditional Labor Day weekend triathlon. Against all odds, he . . .

"Against all odds," he muttered aloud as an unpleasant thought struck. Odds were a hundred to one that it was considered a conflict of interest to participate in a sporting contest on which you were taking bets. Even bookmakers had their ethics, didn't they?

He'd better run the news by Harry.

"Time for a french fry fix?" Harry asked cheerfully as Winston wedged his costume through the doorway. "The better to advertise our wares." He shook the strainer basket full of fries, sending Winston's favorite perfume into the air.

"No, thanks," Winston heard himself say.

Harry whirled around. "You feeling OK?"

"Yep. But I'm in training now. They've made me a member of the squad. I'm sort of replacing Ryan." The words sounded like music to his own ears. "Sort of," he said again, in the interest of truth.

"Hey, that's terrific." Harry pumped Winston's hand. Then a look of concern crossed his face. "Does that mean no more Mr. Hamburger?"

"No, I'm just an honorary member," Winston admitted. "They did it to have enough team members for the triathlon."

"I'm sure your honorary presence on the squad will make Sweet Valley the hands-down favorite," Harry declared. "Hey, Docs," he called out, leaning across the counter toward his table of mustached regulars. "Guess what?"

"Wait a minute," Winston said. "Not so fast. That's the trouble. The gambling, I mean. How can I collect bets on a race I'm in?"

Harry waved away the concern with his usual get-out-of-here gesture. "Lighten up on this 'gambling' business, will you, Winston? We're talking nickels and dimes here. Ice cream cone money, and it's probably better for people than ice cream." He pointed to his soft-serve frozen custard machine. "You ever read the ingredient list on that thing?" he asked dramatically.

"Gambling's still against the law in this state," Winston pointed out.

"Yeah, well, so is walking your dog without a leash," Harry said. "And so are some of my dreams," he added with a sigh, glancing in the direction of two swimsuit-clad girls giggling over sodas. "So relax and enjoy the fun, Winston. What we're doing isn't hurting anyone. It's the original victimless crime. And it's not as though you're really on the squad," he went on. "Try to think of yourself as a mascot."

"Thanks," Winston said glumly. "Maybe I will have those spuds."

He didn't laugh when a little kid with freckles sauntered in and poked him in the roll. For once he didn't feel like being the comic relief.

"I wanna put money on the tri—," the boy began, groping for the word. "The trithumpa-long," he concluded triumphantly.

"Oh, great," Winston muttered with a groan. "We're corrupting infants."

The boy glared at Winston. "I'm thirteen years, two months, and eleven days old," he announced, pulling himself up to his full five feet.

"Even I have to draw a line somewhere," Harry declared. "Sorry, kid, if you're too young to pronounce it, you're too young—" He stopped and cleared his throat, and Winston knew without turning toward the door that some gorgeous girl had walked in.

It was Rachel.

"Oh, hi, Winston," she said with tinsel cheeriness. "So how did your friends take the news about our bet on the triathlon?"

"Triathlong!" the freckle-faced boy exclaimed. "See? I said it. Now can I bet?"

"There's no *g* at the end of it," Harry informed him. "But even if there were, I still don't take bets from anyone under . . . fourteen."

"Why, Harry . . ." Rachel batted her eyelashes. "You're discriminating on the basis of age? And I always thought you were so fair-minded."

"Yeah, I could probably sue you," the boy piped up. "Unless you take this." He waved a five-dollar bill in front of Harry.

Harry clapped a hand to his forehead. "Just what I need, a pint-size lawyer on my case."

"Oh, take his money," Rachel said. "Then maybe you and I can have some time alone, Harry."

Rachel vamping Harry for the second time in a week? Winston wouldn't have believed it if he weren't a witness. Come to think of it, he wasn't sure he believed it anyway.

He had a sinking feeling that Rachel was setting Harry up to be the butt of a joke.

He leaned over the counter as far as his foam padding would permit. "Harry, I smell a trap," he whispered urgently. "Don't fall into it."

"You're just jealous," Harry whispered back. "Stop raining on all my parades, will you? You used to be fun, Winston. What happened?"

He snatched the five-dollar bill from the boy, then practically ordered Winston to go outside with the kid and write down his particulars.

Winston was on the verge of ripping off his costume and throwing the little black book at Harry. But he couldn't afford to—and not just because of the money.

He didn't have friends to spare at the moment. Aside from true-blue Wendy, he was standing on shaky ground. The more he thought about being an honorary member of the squad, the more he felt it as a jab. The other members of the Sweet Valley gang didn't want him to forget for a minute how much was riding on the triathlon.

"OK, kid," he said to the boy. "Let's go."

"Shhh," Paul whispered urgently. "I think he went thataway." He released his grip on Wendy.

"Who?" she whispered back, breathing raggedly. Her head was swimming.

"No time to explain. Come on."

Two tours of the house later Paul shook his head. "I guess he sneaked away."

"Will you tell me what's going on?" Wendy demanded. The dizzy feeling had turned into a plain old headache. Her jeans and white shirt were sticking to her skin. She wanted to drink a pitcher of ice water and then lie down in a dark room with a washcloth over her face.

"I was just passing by and I thought I saw someone sneaking around," Paul said. "I decided to check it out. I guess he got away. Or maybe I just had too much sun today." He flashed his dazzling smile.

They reassured themselves that all the doors were still locked. "Guess I was wrong," Paul said cheerfully. "But I'm not going to leave you until we check the windows."

As they tested the newly repaired kitchen window, Paul pointed inside. "I wouldn't leave that purse on the counter by the phone anymore," he said. "It tempted somebody once. It could tempt them again."

"Yeah, you're right. Thanks, Paul."

"You cool being here alone?" Paul asked.

"I'm not alone. I have Carlos. See you later."

As she watched him walk away Wendy replayed his words in her head. Something wasn't right.

Then she got it, and a thrill of suspicion ran through her. How on earth had he known that her purse had been on the counter by the phone during the first break-in? She hadn't mentioned that detail to anyone but the police.

Much as she hated to admit it to herself, she had a horrible feeling that charming Paul Jackson was the thief.

Chapter Six

Elizabeth sucked in gulps of air as she jogged from the beach house to the lifeguard station. Fall was coming, she could sense it in the lengthening shadows and a hint of coolness beneath the afternoon heat, and she felt a sudden urge to breathe in the essence of summer.

A part of her wished she had never heard of Sweet Valley Shore. This had been a disastrous three months in more ways than one. Yet she loved the briny tang in the air and the rhythmic beat of the waves. In that instant Elizabeth understood the surfers who followed the sun, trying to keep winter forever at bay.

It wasn't just the cold of winter, it was the *old* of winter. Something in her resisted the idea of researching history papers and saving the world and doing all the other serious, grown-up things that lay around the corner. Labor Day was almost at hand, and she felt as if she hadn't yet had a summer vacation.

The poignant strands of "Au Clair de la Lune," one of her favorite songs, drifted up to her. Turning her head as she ran, she saw a great-looking dark-haired hunk strumming a guitar. She sensed that he was aware of her, and for a wild minute she was tempted to drop down onto his beach towel and invite him to sing to her. She would forget about both Tom and Ryan and, oh, everything, and she would squeeze a whole summer into one afternoon.

But of course she couldn't do that because she was the *responsible* Wakefield twin, even in this crazy mixed-up summer, and she had to tell Nina that Captain Feehan was looking for Paul. Ryan wasn't the only mystery guy on the scene, that was for sure.

She ran faster and faster, the sound of the guitar blurring then fading behind her.

Nina's dark eyes combed the water, back and forth. The surf was pounding in a ragged, unpredictable tempo that was making her nervous.

Ryan had taught her how to read the ocean. Each current had its own name and own behavior, just as people did. And he had taught her that sometimes the ocean could not be read. Now and then it seemed to have a mind of its own, its waves moving in an irregular rhythm. This was one of those times. Or perhaps she just wasn't seasoned enough to see the pattern this afternoon.

It was a day to stay extra alert, in any event. The beach was jammed with pleasure seekers.

Nina targeted the people she wanted to keep an extra-alert eye on. A toddler in a blue sun hat who kept wandering off his big plaid blanket toward the edge of the water. His mother had leaped to her feet each time so far, but she had two older kids who might distract her.

Then there was the gangly guy with a surf-board tucked under his arm and audible boasts on his lips about "walking the nose," which meant he wanted his girlfriend to marvel as he balanced on the very tip of his board. And a white-haired, heavyset man who looked alarmingly red—a per-fect candidate for sunstroke. Summer was about to end, and people were determined to play—at al-most any cost.

Elizabeth climbed into the chair to join Nina for the noon shift. "Captain Feehan came by the house while I was there. He said that if we see Paul, we should ask him to drop by the police station."

Nina's heart stumbled. "Did he say why?"

"No."

"Maybe it's about the break-in here and at Pedro's," Nina blurted.

"Do you suspect him?" Elizabeth asked softly.

"I hate to, but I can't *not* suspect him." Nina groaned. "Just the way I can't *not* like him."

Elizabeth sighed hugely. "We sure picked a couple of winners this summer."

They sighed again, then each smiled wanly. Suddenly Nina caught sight of a flimsy inflatable two-passenger boat that made her forget about everything but being a lifeguard.

That boat was in trouble, she was sure of it. Her hands tightened on the reassuringly hard plastic of the red rescue buoy. She nervously fingered its tail-like rope, which lay neatly coiled in her lap. Some lifeguards left the buoy hanging on the arm of the chair. It was an acceptable procedure. But Ryan had always kept it on his lap when he was on duty, and Nina followed his example.

The blond-haired boy and the dark-haired girl in the boat stood up—doing some kind of dance, it looked like.

Nina blew sharply on her whistle to catch their attention, but they ignored her.

She reached for the bullhorn. "Those crazy kids aren't wearing life vests. I think they're gonna—"

She didn't get to finish the sentence. A big wave washed over the little boat, knocking its passengers into the swirling water.

"Let's go!" Nina shouted, blowing a double blast to alert the other lifeguards. Not pausing a minute, she and Elizabeth jumped the five feet drop down to the sand. Elizabeth grabbed the rescue board that was propped against her side of the chair, while Nina adjusted the shoulder strap on the buoy.

They raced toward the surf, intuitively timing

106

the waves, their moves perfectly choreographed. As a wave crested and broke Nina shouted, "Now," and they dove into the water.

Surfacing, they stroked toward the flailing kids. Nina's skin burned from the icy fire of the waves.

"Grab the boat!" she screamed at the kids.

The girl lunged, but the little red craft got caught in cresting foam and swirled out of their reach.

Instinct told Nina that the boy was going to be the tougher save, and she assigned herself to him, ordering Elizabeth to go for the girl. She flung the rescue buoy at the boy. "Catch!" But he disappeared below the surface, and the rubber buoy bobbled like bright driftwood.

"I'm coming!" she heard Elizabeth shout to the girl.

Arms and legs knifing through the water, Nina counted the seconds. It was another trick she'd learned from Ryan. The counting not only let her know how much time the victim had before he asphyxiated, it helped her to ignore the ice and the dread of losing a victim and the fears for her own safety.

Five precious minutes of air. Three hundred little seconds.

She imagined the horror of towing in a dead body instead of a live human being. A limp, heavy form trailing seaweed, never to laugh or kiss or cry again. She stroked with doubly ferocious energy against the surging sea.

Two hundred fifty. Pull . . . two hundred forty. Pull.

Then she was there, miraculously within reach, and she lunged for the boy's terrifyingly inert form. Grabbing an arm, she propelled him back up into the air, only to have him suddenly reanimate and panic.

He kicked her and swung at her with his free hand as if she were a deadly sea creature instead of his last hope.

"I'm going to save you!" she shouted. But he went on struggling.

Nina heaved him up and flipped him onto his side. She threw her left arm around him, pinioning his arms while keeping his head above water. She was dimly aware of Elizabeth and the girl just ahead of them.

"I've got you! You're safe!" she said over and over again to the boy, her right arm paddling for all it was worth toward the shore.

Worn out, he sagged against her. With a shock she realized he was about the same height and weight as Paul.

As they staggered onto the sand Ben and Jessica came running with blankets and towels. The boy shoved them away as he doubled over and puked seawater.

The dark-haired girl sobbed with relief in Elizabeth's arms. "You saved my life! I was going to die, and you saved me! And your friend saved Quinn. How can we ever thank you?"

"By never ever going out in a boat without a life vest again," Elizabeth said.

"I promise," Nina heard the girl sob.

Quinn kicked sand over the mess that his stomach had disgorged, then knelt at the waterline and splashed his face with water. Suddenly he leaped to his feet.

"My boat!" he shouted, pointing.

Nina saw the little red boat. It looked like a toy as it danced atop a wave maybe half a mile away.

The blond guy turned to her. "Get it!" he shrieked. "Go back and get my new boat!"

A rage unlike anything she had ever felt before surged through Nina's body. "Are you crazy?" she shouted. "That boat nearly killed you!"

"Somebody get my boat!" Quinn commanded hysterically, his voice hoarse from vomiting.

A part of Nina knew it was just postshock craziness, but a bigger part of her wanted to throw this unbelievably spoiled monster back into the ocean.

"Go get it yourself, you brat," she snarled. "And this time I'm not coming in after you."

His girlfriend grabbed his arm. "Don't go, Quinn. Don't go!"

"Hey, let him go," Jessica suggested, her hug warming the shivering Nina.

The boy sobbed like a five-year-old as the boat was silhouetted against the horizon for a moment, then disappeared from view.

He turned and grabbed his girlfriend's arm.

"Come on, Jenny." Imperiously tossing a soggy shock of pale hair, he glared at Nina. "I should report you for what you said," he tossed over his shoulder as he stalked off.

Nina and her friends stood openmouthed in disbelief. They'd all had to deal with weird reactions to near drownings before, but this Quinn was in a class by himself.

"I think his ego got a little bruised," Elizabeth said.

"Yeah? Well, I'd like to bruise it again." Nina was nauseated and shaky, the way she always was right after a rescue. The good feeling came later—but today she wasn't sure it was going to come at all. "You OK, Liz?"

"Yep." Elizabeth toweled her hair. "You?"

"I'll live," Nina said. "Especially if someone brings me a cola." All at once she broke into peals of laughter.

"Hello?" Elizabeth tilted her head and hopped to shake water out of her ear.

"I was just thinking of what you said before," Nina answered. "About you and me knowing how to pick them. Even our drowning victims are losers!"

Elizabeth laughed. "Well, the girl was nice enough," she said. "And maybe Paul will turn out to be Mr. Clean."

"Right." Nina sighed. "And maybe the current will reverse itself and bring back Quinn's little red boat. But not even Winston would bet on that."

*　　*　　*

Jessica clapped her hand over her mouth. "Jenny!" she sputtered.

"What?" Ben asked with a quizzical look.

"That was Jenny! As in, 'I love Jenny.'" She pointed to the sky. "Remember?"

Ben laughed. "I wonder what old Quinn's going to have to do today to endear himself to Jenny. She looked pretty disgusted."

"Yeah, well, I know how she feels," Jessica said. "As a former specialist in losers."

Throwing an arm around her shoulders, Ben grinned—a perfectly symmetrical grin that had nothing to do with his famous biting wit. Biting was definitely not what he wanted to do with his wit or his mouth. He pulled Jessica close and gently took off her green baseball cap. Her blond hair tumbled down loosely over her shoulders. He kissed a few locks softly. Their warmth and yellowy brightness seemed like a puddle of sunshine, the essence of summer.

"The word *former* never sounded better," he said. "Except—"

"What?" Jessica asked against his chest.

"I suddenly heard the words *Mrs. Benjamin K. Mercer, the former Jessica Wakefield.*"

The minute the words were out, he was afraid he'd said too much. He glanced over at the lifeguard chairs where Nina and Elizabeth were perched, but they were immersed in quietly scanning the ocean.

111

"Oh, neat," Jessica exclaimed with reassuring lightness. "Does that mean we're, um, engaged to be engaged to be engaged?"

"Gee, a recursive definition," Ben said admiringly. "Right out of the textbook on mathematical logic. I'm impressed. Engaged to be engaged to be engaged is just what I meant."

She pulled out of the embrace to look up at him. "But what if our children have my brains and your looks?"

"Just lucky, I guess," Ben said.

Jessica all but purred. "You really think I'm that smart?"

"No, I just think I'm that good looking," he retorted, fluffing up his short dark hair.

Laughing, she swatted him. "Conceited."

"Yeah, sure am." He stuck out his chest, preening. "Jessica Wakefield's in love with me. I must be pretty hot stuff."

"Let's see how hot you are. Race you to Harry's."

"Deal!" Ben said. Then he had a better idea. "Let's practice for the triathlon. I'll time you to Harry's, then you time me. We can cool down with some swimming laps."

Jessica stretched, flexing her bare feet. Ben suddenly noted with amusement that somehow she'd found time in the last twenty-four hours to change the color of her toenails from pink to red.

"Racing Red?" he asked, pointing. He got a kick out of the names of lipsticks and nail polishes.

"Ruby Romance," Jessica corrected him haughtily. Then she grinned. "Or should I call it Rubric Romance?" Her expression shifted again, to one of determination and focus. "Don't distract me. It's half a mile from the lifeguard station to Harry's. I say I can do it in under three minutes—way under. Two-thirty or bust."

Her muscles rippled under her glowing skin. *She's going to do it,* Ben thought proudly. *Two-thirty today, maybe two twenty-nine tomorrow.*

She drew a line in the sand perpendicular to the chair and dropped down into starting position. Ben put his thumb to the crown of his stopwatch and declared, "On your mark—"

Nina and Elizabeth called down cheers.

"Go!" Ben shouted.

Jessica leaped into the air, propelling herself forward, and came down on the far side of the lifeguard station. Then time seemed to stop as Jessica screamed.

She dropped to the sand, plummeting like a bird brought down by a hunter.

Ben froze with fear. Crazy as the thought was, he could only imagine that Jessica had been shot.

"Jess!" Elizabeth cried hysterically, leaping down from the chair.

"My foot!" Jessica wailed.

As Ben tenderly took her right foot in his hand, he nearly recoiled. Blood gushed from the transverse arch. Just below her middle toe an inch-long gash gaped open horribly.

"Careful, Elizabeth," he urged as she started to root in the sand. "Whatever Jess stepped on is still there."

"I know exactly where it is," Jessica said between sobs. Leaning over, she reached gingerly into the sand.

"A knife?" they all chorused wonderingly a moment later as she pulled it up.

Ben took the knife into his hand, holding it by the cross guard between the handle and the blade. Something was very wrong at Sweet Valley Shore, and it occurred to him that the police might want to dust the handle for fingerprints.

"Please," Jessica sobbed. "Somebody do something."

Nina knelt next to her, unscrewing the top on the bottle of hydrogen peroxide. "This is going to sting, Jess, but I've got to do it. Then we'll get you to the emergency room. I think you're going to need stitches."

Ben offered Jessica his hand. "Go ahead, Jess, dig your nails into my palm. I don't care."

Elizabeth put her arms around her sister.

"Ow! Ow!" Jessica yelped.

"I am going to pulverize whoever left that knife there," Ben swore. "Squeeze harder, Jess. You can't hurt me."

"Is that a challenge?" she asked through her tears, and he shook his head with smiling admiration. On top of everything else, Jessica had a gallant spirit. He wondered if he would ever stop discovering new things to adore in her.

"You're the greatest," he whispered in her ear as Nina taped a loose bandage over the wound. He scooped Jessica up and carried her toward the parking lot.

"I think I'm dripping blood on your trunks," she murmured against his chest. Her sobs had subsided now.

"Don't worry about it," he said tenderly. "They're red. And even if they were white, it wouldn't matter. Am I holding you OK?"

"Perfectly," she murmured in a silky voice. "Were you ever in agony and ecstasy at the same time, Ben? I'd rather be here like this with you than dancing with any other guy."

On top of everything else, she was a poet. He just prayed that the wound wouldn't mean an end to dancing. Or running. He shuddered at the thought of Jessica's proud, strong body compromised in any way.

She had to be all right! He broke into a run, her weight as light as a child's in his loving arms.

"Holy freakout!" Winston babbled. His lips quivered in a hopeful smile. "You're kidding, guys, right? Ha, ha, ha. That was a good one," he said weakly, slapping his thigh.

"Believe me, Winston, we wish it were a joke," Nina said.

"Especially me." Jessica ruefully showed him her heavily bandaged foot.

The Sweet Valley Shore gang were gathered in their living room. It was six o'clock, time for the unwinding hour. The beach was closed and the sun was starting to slip into the western sky, suffusing the air with a golden haze. Everyone had showered off salt and sand and changed into clean jeans and bright tees or sweatshirts. Winston smelled a bouquet of shampoos, and the ice in their glasses tinkled as pleasantly as wind chimes. Even Paloma Perro looked relaxed, a softly snoring heap at Wendy's feet.

"I saw your face when I told you we were making you an honorary member of the squad," Ben said. "I know you hoped it was for real."

"For about thirty seconds," Winston insisted.

"Come on, Winston," Wendy softly urged him. "Live out your hero fantasies."

Winston shot his friends a baleful look. "Thank you, Dr. Freud and Dr. Jung."

"You can wear my lucky pendant," Jessica offered.

"How about I wear your yellow bikini so the South Beach team falls down laughing?" Winston suggested sourly. "Come on, guys," he pleaded. "It's not me I'm worried about. I mean, the fact that I'll probably have a heart attack is a minor detail you shouldn't even think about. But I just don't want to let all of you down."

His face brightened as an idea struck. "What if you asked Captain Feehan to make it teams of seven? We could call it the Lucky Seven Triathlon—pretty catchy, isn't it?"

"Maybe Ryan will come down the chimney," Wendy said.

Nobody laughed.

"Ryan is history." Ben's voice was grim.

"Maybe not," Jessica said. "I bet if you asked him to come back, he'd do it, Liz."

"Jess, what did they give you for painkillers?" Nina groaned. "He's never coming back."

"I'm not so sure," Wendy said. "I mean, maybe he's dying for a chance to prove that he still cares about the squad."

"If he ever did," Winston said glumly, suddenly hating Ryan.

"Of course he cared!" Elizabeth cried hotly. "The big loser," she added.

"Look, he gave me a second chance," Wendy pointed out. "I never thought he'd let me on the squad this summer after kicking me off last summer for being such a joker, but he did. So maybe we should do the same thing for him."

"Maybe you're right," Ben said. "It can't hurt to ask, anyway. Will you try, Liz?"

"Sorry," Elizabeth said flatly. "No way."

"Yes way," Jessica said. "You've got to. It's the only way we can beat that rotten Rachel. Otherwise I'm going to run, no matter what the doctor ordered."

Her sister's eyes opened in horror. "You wouldn't! You could damage your foot for life!"

Jessica tightened her lips.

Elizabeth tightened hers.

Winston decided that this was a very good moment to start working on dinner.

"I'm going out for ice cream," Elizabeth announced after dinner.

"We have a freezer full of ice cream," Nina pointed out. "Chocolate chip cookie dough, Mocha Madness, pineapple-passion fruit sorbet—"

"Remember vanilla?" Elizabeth asked. "I suddenly have a craving for plain old vanilla. From Dairy Dream."

"But that's half an hour away," Jessica said.

"So I feel like driving, OK?" Elizabeth snapped.

All the way to the ice-cream bar she pretended that vanilla was what was mostly on her mind. But when she got back into the car with her double-dipped cone, she didn't head home.

She kept going straight toward Tilton.

This time she didn't hesitate outside the Trail's End Pub. She marched inside, spotted Ryan, and headed determinedly toward him.

"We've got to talk," she said. "I mean, we *have* to."

He sighed none too happily, but something in her voice must have made him realize it was futile to protest.

"I'll get Albert to cover for me," he said. "There's a diner across the street where we can be relatively private."

The diner was a fifties-style place with plastic-covered turquoise banquettes and a menu that featured old-fashioned fare such as meat loaf and rice pudding. The waitress was a motherly woman, also in turquoise, with the name Rose printed on a big name tag. She tried to persuade Elizabeth to have pie, but Elizabeth's stomach was in knots and she was already regretting the vanilla cone, even though she'd tossed it out the car window halfway through. She ordered coffee. Ryan ordered coffee and a brownie with chocolate ice cream and "just a little" hot-fudge sauce.

"Whipped cream?" Rose urged.

Ryan smiled for the first time since Elizabeth had arrived in Tilton. "Stop trying to fatten me up," he ordered. "I'm in training."

"In training for what?" Elizabeth asked pointedly. "For being a waiter?" She knew it was a mean question, but she was tired of pampering him. She kept thinking of Jessica threatening—and probably meaning it—to run with a damaged foot. And what about Winston? And all the money that she and her friends stood to lose. Not to mention the misery of losing to a team that would gloat as mercilessly as South Shore.

"In training for life," Ryan said wearily.

"Really? Or do you mean running *from* life?"

"I know what it looks like, but you don't know the whole story, Elizabeth."

"Then tell it to me!" she said explosively.

Rose delivered their order. Ryan added two sugars to his coffee, then stirred it and stirred it until Elizabeth thought she would scream.

"I can't," Ryan said.

"Or you won't," she replied. She sipped her coffee. "We've got a crisis. OK, not a life-and-death crisis, but a lot of people's happiness is at stake." She filled him in on some of the details—Winston's rash bet, Jessica's injury, the burglaries.

"Do you know how much you mean to us all?" she burst out.

But he sat there impassively, not dropping the stirring spoon from his hand for an instant. "I can't imagine why."

"Nina and Jessica said they could hear your voice when they made their saves this afternoon."

"That makes me feel wonderful," he said sincerely. "But it doesn't change the facts. The *idea* of Ryan Taylor is one thing. The reality is another."

"What are you afraid of?"

"Of me, dammit." He slapped the Formica table for emphasis, and coffee from his untasted cup slopped over the edge. "There," he said, mopping the spill with his napkin. "Are you satisfied?"

"No," she said calmly. "That's just another tease. It's not an answer."

"Sometimes there are no answers," Ryan said.

"You should eat your ice cream," she said. "Unless you like chocolate puddles." As he obediently stuck a spoon into his dessert she took a bold stab.

"I had a long talk with Captain Feehan this morning," Elizabeth said. "He doesn't blame you for the drowning last summer. He's still haunted by the accident—he says everyone is because there's nothing worse than losing a child. But that hasn't kept him from doing his job. If anything, it's made him do his job even better."

She leaned forward, fixing Ryan's gaze. She knew that something important was at stake here—more important than their relationship or the triathlon. "So why don't you put what you learned to use instead of feeling sorry for yourself?"

"I know it looks like self-pity," Ryan said quietly. "But you'd blame me too, if you knew the whole story."

For a brief moment he reached across the table to touch Elizabeth's hand. "I know what it took for you to come back here today, and I'm really grateful. I care about you, Elizabeth. That's why I want you to turn around and drive back to the beach and forget about me."

His eyes shifted, and Elizabeth traced his gaze to the window. The pretty red-haired young woman from last night was standing across the street in front of the Trail's End Pub, looking at her watch.

"I have to go," Ryan said hurriedly. Piercing Elizabeth with a brief, regretful look, he got up and then was gone.

*   *   *

Wendy's heart leaped when she opened the door and saw the huge basket of tropical flowers on the stoop. Who but Pedro could have put together this extravagant riot of color and shape— lavender orchids, waxy red anthuriums, and velvety yellow puffs that looked as if they'd grown on Mars?

"Surprise!" Paul yelled, jumping out from behind a bush. "Is Nina home?"

"We have to stop meeting this way," Wendy said with a forced joviality.

Where, oh where, was Pedro? And what was she going to do about the fact that Paul increasingly gave her the creeps?

Nina leaned in the doorway, arms folded tightly across her chest. She didn't invite Paul in.

"Jessica's the one who should have flowers," she said coldly. "After the trauma of stepping on a knife outside the lifeguard station." She didn't add that it was a diving knife, just like the one Paul owned—a thought that had been burning her brain ever since Jessica's accident.

Paul bounded up the steps like the jaunty star of a musical comedy. He plucked a fragrant stem of white freesia out of the sumptuous flower basket.

"For Ms. Jessica Wakefield, with my compliments," he said, bowing gallantly. "But the rest are for the beautiful Nina Harper. The florist said they should be refrigerated at night—but then again, she didn't know what a chilly reception they were going to get. What's up?"

Doubts flooded Nina's mind. The relentlessly cheerful guy in the cream-colored V-neck sweater just didn't sound or look like someone whose knife had hurt another human being—even accidentally.

Still, she couldn't take a chance. She'd taken too many already.

"I'm sorry, Paul, I can't accept any more presents from you," she declared.

He threw back his head and laughed. "Oh, I get it," he said. "You're afraid I'm trying to undermine your steely will to blow me away in the triathlon? Yeah, I can see how that would be a problem."

"No, Paul—"

He held up a hand, cutting off her words. "Hey, it's cool. I kind of like that in you—that you can't handle being competitive with the man in your life. Makes me feel you take me seriously, you know? The romance is on hold until the end of Labor Day weekend . . . and may the best lifeguard win."

He blew her a kiss, jumped down the front steps, and disappeared into the night, leaving Nina staring openmouthed.

She'd known her share of arrogant men, but this had to be the cockiest guy on the planet. Wouldn't she just love to take the wind out of *his* sails!

Her mind whirled. Somehow the Sweet Valley Shore team had to set a trap, prove him a crook, and get him disqualified. That way they would be even. They might not have Jessica, but South Shore wouldn't have Paul.

She went back into the house, calling Jessica's name. "You've got to come up with a plan," she declared. "We've just got to get Paul."

"Yeah, Jess," Winston said. "Plotting always was your number-one sport."

"And if it was his knife you stepped on, he should be your number-one enemy," Nina said.

"Tied with Rachel," Ben pointed out.

Jessica rubbed her hands together. "Team, it will be a pleasure."

Chapter Seven

"Hello, gorgeous," Jessica said into the mirror.

She was in a very good mood. It was lots of fun being officially allowed to scheme and lie.

She alternately held up two shirts—a crisp white linen button-down styled like a safari jacket, complete with epaulets, and an oversize green smock that made up for in sheerness what it lacked in shape. Which one made her look more innocent?

Neither one, she decided. She discarded both shirts in favor of a loosely knit sweater the color of faded jeans.

Yes, in this one she could get away with almost anything, she decided. It played up the gold of her hair, making her look as innocent as a cornfield under a cloudless sky.

She had to admit that it would be fun to lie again. After all, lying was—or had been—one of her major talents. She was like a great opera singer who was being given a chance to go onstage again after a summer of voicelessness.

The funny thing was, the summer had begun with a whopper. She'd told a nameless, arrogant pest in an oversize T-shirt and a baseball cap that she wasn't the slightest bit interested in him—because she already had a boyfriend. The supposed boyfriend was Ryan Taylor, and the pest had turned out to be Ben Mercer. After her plan to break Elizabeth and Ryan apart failed miserably, she'd had to admit the truth—to herself and then to Ben. Pretty soon she'd figured out that Ben was worth a hundred Ryans, and she hadn't lied to herself or to him since.

It wasn't just that he was too smart to be suckered. He was also the easiest person in the world to be honest with. He might tease her when she was silly, but he never made her regret a revelation about her past follies or present feelings.

"And honesty is good for you," she campily added to the audience in the mirror. "Yes, honesty is broccoli for the soul. So try some. You'll be glad you did."

She brushed her hair, glossed her lips, considered mascara, and decided against it.

Now she just had to go to the bank for a big wad of cash—her prop. And then on to South Beach to lie her head off in a noble cause: the pride and prosperity of Sweet Valley Shore.

Jessica smiled. *It's good to be back.*

*　　*　　*

"Doesn't it make you nervous, having all this cash around?" Winston asked Harry. "Especially after back-to-back robberies in the neighborhood? Look, that window's wide open."

"Nah," Harry said with one of his magisterial waves. "First of all, nothing makes me nervous, as you oughta know by now. Second of all, this part of the building sticks out over the water, remember? You think some James Bond type in diving gear is going to rise up out of the depths? Besides, there aren't many characters brave or desperate enough to face the chaos of this room."

"Harry, calling this 'chaos' is like calling a hamburger chopped steak. This room is a pigsty."

The only place to sit was a gray-sheeted bed that was never made. The bureau boasted four overflowing drawers and a cracked mirror. Neither of the two TV sets worked, the desk was piled almost to the ceiling with papers, the floor appeared to be littered with cat food—and Harry didn't even have a cat.

Still, Winston had to admit that the betting book seemed to be in pretty good order, and the crumpled singles and five-dollar bills in the cash box added up just right.

"I'm an honest crook," Harry said cheerfully. "You satisfied? If so, I'd appreciate it if you scrammed. I'd like to get ready for my date with Rachel." He flapped his eyebrows, and Winston cringed. Harry on a date with Rachel was like a blowfish going out with a shark—not a pretty picture.

"So, Har—" he started, then stopped. The freckle-faced thirteen-year-old was standing at the doorway, waving a fistful of dollars.

"Hi, guys," the kid said.

"Don't tell me you smashed another piggy bank?" Harry asked with a grimace. "Forget it, sonny."

"Why should I?" the boy whined. "It's my money. I can do whatever I want with it."

"Not here, you can't. Sorry. Five bucks was one thing, but this is too much."

The kid wiped his nose with the back of his hand. "You let me bet as much as I want, or I'm telling the police that you're a bookie."

"Me—a bookie?" Harry squeaked. "What are you talking about? Well, what the heck, give me your money. Write it down, Winston."

"It goes on Sweet Valley," the kid said.

"I know, I know," Winston muttered.

When the kid left, whistling, Winston looked at Harry. Judging from the beads of sweat on his friend's forehead, Harry was close to panic.

Harry wasn't the only one, that was for sure. Winston might have fainted—if the prospect of fainting onto Harry's bed or floor weren't so horrifying.

The kid was blackmailing them and the stakes were getting higher!

This was one screwup that Winston wasn't

going to be able to talk himself out of. Good-bye, Denise. Good-bye, college career. Good-bye, everything!

"Look what the wind blew in," Tina commented as Jessica hobbled into the South Beach lifeguard station. "If you came to see your dear friend Rachel, she's otherwise occupied," Tina added with a little snicker.

"Chill, Tina," Paul advised. "Jessica's obviously in pain. I bet she came with a scented little note from a certain someone in her house, am I right?"

"I just came to bask in the famous South Beach warmth," Jessica said, dripping sweetness.

"Seriously, Jess, I'm sorry about your foot," Paul said. "It looks really painful." His own feet were up on the driftwood coffee table that was the centerpiece of the room. The South Beach lifeguard station had much more of a clubhouse feeling than its strictly business Sweet Valley counterpart.

"Yeah, it hurts like crazy," Jessica said. "But the worst part is the boredom. I can't work. I can't run. I can't swim. I'm not even allowed to drive—I got Ben to drop me off. That's why I thought I'd check you guys out. And since it's the end of summer, I thought maybe we should patch up our differences."

Nobody said anything for a moment, and Jessica was afraid she'd gone too far and made them suspicious. Then Kyle put down his magazine and smirked.

"Are you sure it was your foot that took the hit and not your head?" he asked.

"Yeah, you're right, I do sound weird," Jessica admitted with a relieved laugh. "The truth is, I came here to plant a bug so we could know your secret strategy for the triathlon." Opening her straw shoulder bag, she pretended to root around inside for something small.

"You know what we do to spies?" big, blond Danielle asked. She made a wringing motion with her hands.

"Eeek!" Jessica exclaimed. "I don't think I want to find out."

She stood up in haste, grabbed her bag, and swung it over her shoulder—and out poured its entire contents.

"Oh no!" Jessica cried. "I'm such a klutz!" But inside she was cheering. As she scrambled to reclaim her wallet, hairbrush, cosmetics, and a tissue packet, all eyes were on another item—a rubber-banded wad of ten-dollar bills.

"Which bank did you rob, Jess?" Tina asked.

"Actually I robbed my own account at First America," Jessica said. "I wanted to buy something for my mom at a shop in Tilton that doesn't take checks. But then this thing happened to my foot, so I can't drive. I should really put the money back in the bank. But I guess it's too late now. I'll just have to do it tomorrow." Pretending to shudder, she added, "If I don't get robbed first."

130

"Can't we be civilized about this?" Wendy asked. "I don't love you any the less just because I love him. Do you understand?"

With a fine disregard for her words, Paloma Perro jumped out of her arms and made a beeline for Carlos's dish.

She wondered what had possessed her to get the two dogs together. Did she really think they could be friends? Was it just in case, by some wonderful, miraculous chance, they might live under the same roof one day?

It seemed as if Pedro were very far away. A shared future was impossibly far off. That was the sort of wishful thinking the horrible girls from South Beach had accused her of.

"No, Paloma!" she cried in exasperation. "I already fed you, don't you remember? Oh, you're hopeless!" she exclaimed as he nudged aside the more gentlemanly Carlos.

Picking up Paloma and grasping him firmly, she tried to encourage Carlos back to his bowl. But she'd come to Pedro's house an hour earlier than she usually did, and the well-trained Carlos tended to be hungry by the clock. Or perhaps he was being a gracious host, as his master always was, and didn't want to eat unless his visitor did.

She'd already fed Paloma, but maybe a little snack would calm him down.

She was on the way to the kitchen when the telephone rang.

Carlos barked. Paloma barked. The answering machine picked up, and Wendy adjusted the volume so she could have the thrill of hearing Pedro's outgoing message. Two G-major chords on the guitar, then the world's most fabulous voice.

*This is Pedro Paloma's
recorded voice.
Leave word or hang up;
You have a choice.*

*But if you hang up,
it's plain to see,
you won't get a call
ba-a-ack from me.*

*So leave a message
after the tone,
and soon you'll hear me
on your phone.*

Before she could turn the volume down or move out of earshot to protect his privacy, she heard a cheerful twang.

"Hey, man. It's Seth. I hope you've enjoyed being a beach bum for a week because I've got another tour lined up. Can you believe it? Strike while the iron is hot, that's the rule in this biz. I've booked ten days in the Northeast—Montreal, Boston, Hartford, and New York. Yup, that's right, the Big Apple. It's not Madison Square

Garden, not this time, but we're heading that way, believe me. Call me, and plan to get lots of R and R over the Labor Day weekend."

Wendy sank down onto the couch, then bounced up again. She had to have misheard—had to! She pressed the playback button, turned up the volume, and listened attentively.

"I hope you've enjoyed being a beach bum for a week . . ."

A week? The tour had been over for a week, and Pedro's very own agent thought he'd been at Sweet Valley Shore all that time?

She grabbed Carlos. "Where is your master, Carlos?" she cried out. "Come on, pooch, tell me— I can take it. He just couldn't say no to all his groupies, is that it?" Carlos's sleek hide was soggy, and Wendy realized she was weeping.

Both dogs started to bark like crazy. All thoughts of groupies fled Wendy's mind. The burglar! Maybe the burglar was back.

She ran to the door and flung it open. Paloma streaked outside toward . . . Rachel!

"Nice dog," Rachel said through clenched teeth. But she couldn't keep the look of distaste from her face as she patted the riotous fur.

"What are you doing here?" Wendy asked coldly.

"I came to drop off a note for Pedro," Rachel answered with a smirk. "I believe that's a legal act in the state of California."

Wendy didn't rise to the bait. She held out her hand. "I'll take it."

"Sure." Thrusting her fingers into the pockets of her tight jeans, Rachel seemed surprised that they came up empty. "Gee, I must have dropped it somewhere."

"Uh-huh." Wendy snapped her fingers. "Come on, Paloma. Party's over. Let's go inside."

Rachel didn't take the hint. "You can just pass on the message to your employer, if you're not overwhelmed by your canine duties. Tell Pedro that he's invited to South Beach's post-triathlon victory party. He'll be my personal guest."

"Oh, wow, your *personal* guest," Wendy mocked. "What a thrill. Right up there with being invited to perform at the White House. I don't work for Pedro, as you know perfectly well, but I'll be happy to pass on that very important message to my boyfriend."

Rachel's look turned pitying. "Poor little plain Jane, you really are deluded, aren't you? Well, Pedro certainly snagged the right person. You're here every day, faithful as the tides, ready to do all the scut work. The least he can do is pay you enough so you can have a makeover. You know, they can inject something in your lips so they're actually three dimensional, and I hear the pain only lasts a few days. Men hate thin lips," she added, practically turning her own inside out to show off their fullness.

Wendy's mocking coolness gave way to blatant rage. "Get off Pedro's grounds!" she snarled.

"Spoken like a true caretaker," Rachel said,

turning on her heel. "Don't forget to water the lawn—those brown patches are awfully unsightly, and I'd hate for you to get fired."

Jessica tensed. Was that a scratching at the window she heard?

"Ben, wake up," she whispered urgently.

"Not asleep," Ben slurred. "C'm'ere."

She moved an inch closer and snuggled into his embrace. "There's nowhere else for me to go *but* here," she whispered, then put her hand over his mouth. "Listen."

They were in a cocoon that they'd created by zipping two sleeping bags together. They were lying on the living-room floor behind the sofa, giving themselves a view of the windows on both the front and side of the house. Along with everyone else in the house they'd been on alert all night—well, more or less alert—in the hope of catching Paul when he broke in to steal the cash in Jessica's bag.

"Just wind," Ben announced. He yawned. "What time is it?"

"Look, there's a streak of light in the sky," Jessica pointed out. "I haven't seen dawn since New Year's Eve. I love the way the air smells this early in the morning."

Ben yawned again and tightened his hold on her. "Very poetic, Jess. But what do you say we get five minutes' sleep?"

"You mean you think he's not coming?"

"According to the latest FBI statistics, only three percent of burglaries are committed after first light."

She elbowed him—an easy task, given their proximity. He retaliated by tickling her armpit.

As their giggles filled the air Nina called out in protest from her post by the dining-room windows. "Those of us who are sleeping alone would appreciate a little decorum."

"We're not sleeping," Jessica called back.

"Exactly," Nina retorted.

"I think I fell asleep," Elizabeth confessed.

"That's OK. You didn't miss anything except Ben snoring," Jessica said.

"I didn't!" Ben protested.

"Did too."

Winston and Wendy staggered in from the kitchen, rubbing their eyes.

"Wasn't that exciting?" Winston asked. "I especially liked the part where he drew a pizza cutter on me, and I had to save us all by pouring hot tomato sauce over his head."

"Sounds like a great dream," Jessica said. "Wendy, you look terrible."

Without a word Wendy turned and fled upstairs.

"That was totally jerky, Jess." Winston glared at her.

Jessica was openmouthed. "What did I do? All I meant was that she looked bleary and red eyed—the way we all do, I guess. My hair probably looks like a dust mop."

"Don't flatter yourself," Ben said.

"You know how sensitive Wendy is about her appearance," Winston went on.

"But she's beautiful!" Jessica exclaimed. "I thought Pedro got her past all that insecure stuff."

"Well, he did and he didn't," Winston said evasively. "I'm not saying any more, but just watch it for the next few days, OK?"

Winston's no-fail home fries were a failure. The parts that crisped stuck to the pan, and the parts that didn't stick were rubbery. Adding salt to the tasteless mass just made it taste like fried salt.

"What a bummer," Winston said, noisily chiseling away at an equally wretched second batch with his spatula. "I finally have the perfect high-school science project, but I'm not in high school anymore." He scraped with a vengeance.

"Winston, stop," Nina begged, clasping her ears. "That's worse than chalk on a blackboard."

"Tastes worse too," Ben said. "Nice toast, though—if you're into cardboard."

Winston slammed down the skillet.

"Well, why don't you take over, Chef Ben?" he snapped. "I seem to remember that you have a real knack for opening cereal boxes."

"Please, everybody," Jessica begged. She looked from one of her crumpled housemates to another. "What are you all so crabby about? I feel great, except for my foot."

"Oh, nothing's bothering us, Jess," Elizabeth grated. "It's just that you can't run and Winston can't either. We didn't catch the thief, nobody got any sleep last night, and we're all starving. Other than that, life's a bowl of cherries, so go ahead and pick one."

Chapter
Eight

"Well, you're all up bright and early," Captain Feehan said heartily as he entered the beach-house kitchen.

"Early, yeah, but I don't know about the bright part," Winston replied from his perch by the stove. He was now making his famous slow-scrambled eggs. Very slow this morning, Nina's growling stomach had noticed. "Want some coffee? Or are you on duty? I'll only offer you home fries if you came to arrest me. They're terrible."

"Coffee would be great," Captain Feehan said. "Milk, no sugar. Speaking of being on duty, who's in the lifeguard chair this morning? Can't say any of you looks exactly alert—except for you, Jessica. And I know you're off the roster."

Nina sat up even straighter. "I've got Marcus and Paula on the first shift," she said crisply.

"While Wendy and Ben sleep. No lifeguard's nodding out on *my* watch."

Captain Feehan nodded approvingly. "Good work, Nina. I knew you wouldn't let me down. Oh, by the way, I'm not making any judgments until I hear your side of the story, but I did have a complaint about you. A certain Quinn Daley told me that you threatened to let him drown if he got into trouble."

"That loser!" Elizabeth sputtered. "She saved his life!"

"He's absolutely right," Nina said quietly. "I did tell him that if he went back in, he was on his own. It was the only way I could scare him into staying out of the water. Was there a better way, Captain Feehan?"

The officer took off his sunglasses and polished them thoughtfully. "What do you think, Nina? Was there?"

She looked downward. "I once saw Ryan deal with this guy who jumped into the water with his hands tied behind his back because he was trying to prove he was the new Houdini. He couldn't get the ropes untied, and Ryan had to pull him out. Then he made the guy sit in the lifeguard chair and watch all the little kids building sand castles down by the tide line. He told the guy that what he'd done was as irresponsible as pulling a false alarm. Because what if one of those kids had gotten into trouble while Ryan was saving this guy who deliberately put himself at risk?"

"And was Ryan's approach effective?" Captain Feehan asked. "Did the wannabe Houdini come to his senses?"

"I'll say. He sent Ryan a postcard from Kauai saying he'd enrolled in a lifesaving class. I guess that would have been the way to go with Quinn." She suddenly felt sick inside. "I had no business saying what I did. We don't only save a certain kind of people. All lives are precious."

"Don't you dare be mad at yourself!" Elizabeth said staunchly. "He was a spoiled rich kid who cared more about his little boat than about you—or himself. You did the right thing, Nina."

"But I'm the head lifeguard," Nina said. "Or at least I was," she added with a pleading look at Captain Feehan. She choked back tears of shame. "It would have been bad enough if one of you guys did it, but I'm supposed to set the tone on the beach. I'm supposed to make it feel safe—for everyone."

Loyal Elizabeth looked aghast as she turned to Captain Feehan. "You're not going to demote Nina, are you, Captain? She's the best! No one else could have kept us together after Ryan left." Her voice took on a bitter timbre as she uttered Ryan's name. "You know she would have saved Quinn a second time. And a third time. However many times it took until he got bored with trying to drown."

"Yeah, but Quinn didn't know that," Nina

said. Somehow it only made it harder to hear Elizabeth talk about how wonderful she was. A reputation for being wonderful was a privilege and it carried burdens. It wasn't a license.

"Come on, Nina," Jessica cried. "You're a lifeguard, not a guardian angel. Mother Teresa would have blown her stack at that guy. I bet Jenny breaks up with him for being such a macho dork. He was taking his stupidity out on you."

"Well, you certainly have a fan club, Nina," Captain Feehan said. "And you can still count me as a card-carrying member. I think you learned a valuable lesson. And Quinn probably learned one too." He smiled. "For your information, I told him that he would do well to focus on how lucky he was to be alive. Your position as head lifeguard was never in jeopardy. Thanks for the coffee, Winston."

Captain Feehan was almost at the door when he turned around. "By the way, has anyone seen Paul?" he asked with elaborate casualness.

"You still haven't found him?" Nina asked. The sickening feeling returned.

"Nope."

"Do you want to talk to him about the burglaries?" she blurted.

Captain Feehan hesitated. His lips compressed into a thin line.

"Yes," he said.

Winston glared at Nina and Elizabeth. "Now, look, I know the potatoes were a disaster and the toast was worse, but the eggs reaffirm my status as one of the ten great scramblers in Southern California. Eat!"

"Too bad we can't enter you in a scramblethon," Nina said, listlessly pushing her fork through the mass of bright yellow food on her plate.

"Perfect curds. Perfect!" Winston proclaimed. He enthusiastically swallowed a mouthful of his creation.

The three of them were sitting at the kitchen table. Snores could be heard from elsewhere in the house. Even Jessica had suddenly conked out on the couch, toe to toe with Ben. But Elizabeth and Nina were too unhappy to sleep. Or eat.

Elizabeth patted Winston's hand. "Now's not the time for cooking lessons," she said kindly. "Nina and I need life lessons."

"You do? But you're perfect," Winston declared. Maybe it was his own underslept state, but he suddenly felt very sentimental. His friends were the greatest, and no one was going to knock them—not even themselves.

"Thanks, Winston," Nina said. "But don't you see? Elizabeth and I are, well, perfect curds. I mean, just look at the guys we fell for this summer—a thief and a quitter."

"Are you sure they're that bad?" Winston asked. "Maybe they're just, um, testing you or something. Maybe they're really good eggs, heh, heh."

Elizabeth's blue-green eyes brightened a little. "You know what, Nina? Maybe he's right. Aren't we giving up too easily? Admit it, we're two of the smartest girls we know. So if we fell for those guys, they must have some redeeming qualities."

"Yeah," Winston said enthusiastically. "Great guys. Just because they're tall and athletic and cool and mysterious is no reason for you to hate them. Only for *me* to hate them. Just kidding," he added hastily. "I trust your instincts. So should you."

"Well, thanks for the support," Nina said.

"But you have to admit, it's all so complicated. For both of us," Elizabeth said.

"I mean, how would you have felt if you'd been attracted to someone other than Denise?" Nina chimed in. "Would you have kissed her? And then would you have hated yourself? Or not kissed her and wondered forever what you'd missed?"

He shook his curly head. "Nah. Denise is the only woman for me. But what about you, Liz? What really happened with you and Ryan? Was it a love connection or what?"

"You know what?" Elizabeth said. "I'm going to find out. Once and for all."

She kissed Winston on the forehead, thanked him for breakfast, and grabbed the keys to the Jeep.

Elizabeth turned the air conditioning up full blast and made not one but two stops for coffee and a stretch in the hour-long drive to Tilton. Smart girls didn't fall asleep at the wheel.

At the second stop she dialed information. She knew that an information operator might not give out an address if asked directly, so she used a trick she'd learned from being an investigative reporter.

"In Tilton, I'd like the phone number for Ryan Taylor on Hibiscus Way," she said.

"I don't show any Taylor on Hibiscus Way, but I have a Ryan Taylor on Nelson Place," the operator replied. "Would you like that number?"

"Yes, please," Elizabeth said. A minute later she redialed information, praying that she wouldn't get the same operator. She was in luck. "May I please have the phone number for Ryan Taylor at 101 Nelson Place?" she asked.

"I show a Ryan Taylor at 84 Nelson Place," the operator said. "Hold on for that number—"

Elizabeth didn't hold on. "Eighty-four Nelson," she repeated to herself as she got back into the car.

For a guilty moment she remembered that Tom had taught her that trick for conjuring an address—but there was no room for such feeling today. She was on the hunt for truth, and in a weird way Tom would even approve. He didn't like unanswered questions any more than she did.

Baloney, a voice in her head answered. *He'd be devastated and you know it. You're taking a major chance. This could mean the end of everything with Tom.*

Her stomach tightened, and tears prickled behind her eyes, but she had to press on.

Pulling the Jeep to a halt in front of Ryan's building, she let out the breath she hadn't realized she had been holding. The white-frame five-story building was ramshackle in a beachy sort of way, its facade sun blistered and peeling. But it had a sweet garden and meandering front walk that kept it from being the depressing hideaway she'd been dreading.

But she wasn't here to review the local ambience. She was here to find out what Ryan was made of.

She marched up the front walk and studied the column of bells with their handwritten name cards. Sanderson . . . Richards . . . Khan-Bennett . . . Taylor.

She rang the bell.

He buzzed back immediately.

She was so startled by the instant response that she forgot to push open the door before the buzzing stopped and had to ring again. There was a small, round, perforated intercom speaker, but Ryan hadn't bothered to ask who was there. Was he expecting someone else—the pretty redheaded girl whom Elizabeth had spotted on both her previous visits?

Stop thinking, Wakefield. Just move it before you lose your nerve.

His name had been under the top bell, so she bounded up to the fifth floor. There were two doors, one labeled 5-E, one labeled 5-W. She stood frozen between them. "East, west, what's best?" she asked herself inanely.

Suddenly the door to 5-E opened.

"Elizabeth!"

"Ryan!"

She had never seen a face more explicitly torn apart by emotion. His lips were parted for a kiss, but his eyes were stormy with rejection.

"Well?" she asked with a breeziness she didn't remotely feel. "Are you going to take me in your arms or slam the door in my face?"

For a moment they stood in tense silence.

"Neither one," he said finally, slumping against the doorframe. In his black T-shirt and faded jeans he looked decadent and rebellious but in a soft, old-fashioned way.

"Then how about inviting me in and offering me a glass of cold water?" she suggested. "I ran up the stairs."

"Room-temp water," he corrected peremptorily, for a blessed moment sounding like the all-knowing head lifeguard indoctrinating his rookies.

"Whatever." Elizabeth shook her head.

He opened the door and stood back silently to let her pass into the small living room. They stood there for an awkward moment. "Make yourself at home," he added with a wooden formality.

She wanted desperately to sit down, but the big green armchair—the kind you practically disappeared into—would isolate her. If she sat on the prim tweed sofa, however, it might look as if she were inviting Ryan to cozy up. There were no other choices except for the gray swivel desk chair that belonged in an accountant's office.

Like Ryan's old quarters in the lifeguard station, the room was tidy and spare, offering few clues to the nature of its inhabitant. Even the books seemed to have been acquired for their physical properties. They fit perfectly between the two silent stereo speakers on the single white shelf attached to the wall with angle irons.

She was still standing, dreamily tracing the swirl of dust motes in a shaft of pale light, when Ryan returned. He handed her a glass. Two small ice cubes were swimming in it.

"It's cold!" she said, sipping gratefully.

Ryan shrugged. "I decided, who am I to tell you how to drink your water?"

"You're Ryan Taylor, head lifeguard."

"Former head lifeguard. Will you get that through your head, Liz?"

"It's hard to," she admitted. "My head keeps saying, 'Does not compute.'"

She drained her water glass. "What should I do with this? I don't want to leave a ring on your coffee table."

"It's OK—the owner polyurethaned it," Ryan said. He took the glass and set it down on the table. Now there was nothing between them but air.

A voice inside her head urged her to run before

she made a complete fool of herself. Then she remembered that making a fool of herself was exactly what she'd come to do. Being dignified hadn't gotten her anywhere. Besides, there was nothing to lose. It wasn't as if she were about to jeopardize some great relationship.

"Who is she, Ryan?"

He drew in a long breath of air and smiled a shaky smile. "Just a friend," he answered.

"Have you known her a long time?" Elizabeth pressed. "Where did you meet her?"

"Liz, I really don't want to talk about her."

"But why? If you're in love with somebody else, why don't you just tell me and put me out of my misery?"

"This isn't going to do either of us any good. You'd better go."

"I don't want to go!"

A panicky look crossed his face. "It's my house—you play by my rules. No more questions, got that?" Then he burst out, "Why don't you give up? What do you want from me?"

"I thought you said no more questions." She couldn't resist throwing his words back at him.

He didn't smile. "It's my turn now."

The courage that had gotten her this far suddenly faltered.

"I want you to come back and help us," she cried, then hated her cowardice.

What she really wanted was to shake him out of the daze he'd been in since he'd left Sweet Valley

Shore. She wanted him to be real with her, push her over one edge or the other—love her or leave her. The mixed messages he was sending were driving her crazy.

"I care about you," she said quietly. "Don't you care anything about me?"

His answer was to take her in his arms. As his spicy scent filled her nostrils and his body heat pressed through her thin summer clothes, she felt as if she were being turned inside out and upside down.

Ryan lifted her off her feet, and she was floating above the world in defiance of the known laws of physics. His lips closed in on hers, and the kiss was all there was—sun and moon and stars, oceans and mountains, past and future, good and evil; everything.

"I do care about you, Elizabeth," he whispered, so softly that she might have imagined it. But his tender hands in her hair and his searching lips said that the words were true, no matter how afraid he was to say them.

"Oh, Ryan!" The words seemingly ripped out of her of their own volition. "Kiss me."

"I am kissing you," he said against her cheeks, laughing tenderly at her greed.

"Then never stop kissing me."

They tumbled onto the tweed sofa, lips locked together. She was drowning, but it was drowning into life, not death, and she didn't resist the knowing, masterful hands that moved possessively up and down her body. As long as Ryan wasn't afraid, she wasn't afraid. It was that simple.

So this was what it was all about. This was what surrender meant—the yes that came from so deep inside one's being that there was no arguing with it.

But Ryan broke away. A chill passed over her as she felt him retreat into himself.

"You're a great girl," he whispered hoarsely. "You deserve way better than somebody like me."

"I want you, whatever you are!" Elizabeth cried out.

He kissed her once more—briefly, sorrowfully. "I have to go." He cupped her chin in his hand. "I have an appointment."

"Should I wait for you?" she asked. "Please," she begged shamelessly.

He shook his head. "I can't let you do that to yourself."

"Will you tell me where you're going?" she pleaded. "I want to understand you, Ryan."

"I want to understand myself," he returned passionately. "Can't you see that? I have to get my life settled before I can let anyone else into it."

In numb silence she followed him down the stairs and out the front door of his building. He turned, gripped her shoulders, and uttered three words that tore through her like a knife.

"Forget about me."

He rushed off toward Main Street, not once glancing back. When he was almost out of sight, she realized with a panicky start that if she didn't keep the momentum going, she would never find it again.

I can't let him walk away like that, she told herself. *I just can't. Whatever his secret is, I can handle it. The one thing I can't handle is not knowing.*

Chapter
Nine

Jessica exchanged astonished glances with Nina and Ben as Winston urged his bike across their improvised finish line.

They were in the lush semitropical park where the biking part of the triathlon was going to take place. They'd been timing each other, and the news was good.

"That was amazing!" Jessica shouted as Ben's stopwatch confirmed what they'd all seen with their own eyes. When Winston Egbert put his pedal to the metal, he was faster than Nina and almost as fast as Ben.

"I wouldn't believe it if I hadn't seen it," Nina said, clapping a sweaty but grinning Winston on the back.

Jessica and Ben grinned at each other. Jessica closed her eyes, leaned on Ben's shoulder, and visualized airline tickets fluttering around them like beautiful butterflies.

"Your faith is, as always, touching," Winston said. He took a few sips from his water bottle, then upended the remainder over his head. "Imagine what I can do when I've slept the night before."

"It's your fault if we don't believe in you, Winston Egbert!" Jessica said. "You're always telling us what a slug you are."

"How about if you all take turns giving me deep-muscle massages," Winston suggested. He flopped down onto the grass next to his bike. "Anybody who wants to start now is welcome to. Especially Nina of the famously talented hands."

Nina promptly knelt down next to him, unceremoniously peeled up his soggy blue T-shirt, and pressed her thumbs expertly into the muscles to either side of his neck. As she made bigger and bigger circular motions Winston began to groan.

"Oh, that hurts so good," he declared. "More."

"Breathe," Nina instructed, leaning into him. "Big breaths."

Winston suddenly shrieked. "What are you doing?"

"Shhh. You're a mass of knots. Let me work on them." She sat astride Winston, her long Lycra-striped legs on either side of him. "You didn't get those knots riding a bike, Winston. Are you worried about something?"

"What, me worry?" Winston mumbled. "Harry says we're going to clean up—I'm never going to have to worry again."

Jessica saw Ben's shoulders tense.

"What do you mean, 'clean up'?" Ben asked.

Winston got noticeably silent for a minute.

"Oh, Harry wants to organize a campaign to clean up the boardwalk," he said. "Did you ever notice all that litter stuck in the cracks between the boards? A real eyesore," he brightly chattered on. "Harry's a slob himself, but he can't stand—"

"Nina, get him in a headlock," Ben ordered. "I don't like the sound of this. Come on, Winston. Tell me the sinking feeling in my stomach isn't justified."

"What's going on?" Jessica asked. "I don't get it."

"Enlighten her, Winston," Ben said. "Unless my underslept imagination is running away with me."

"It's no big deal, Jess," Winston said. "Just one of Harry's, um, diversions. You know, anything to entertain the multitudes and make a buck."

"We know *you*," Nina said. She began to pound his spine with the sides of her hands. "What is it this time, Winston?"

"Nina, you're taking totally unfair advantage of me," Winston lamented. "Abusing your power as an unlicensed shiatsu masseuse—"

"For Pete's sake, out with it!" Ben demanded. "How exactly are you and Harry going to clean up?"

"Chill, Ben. All we did was take a little action on the triathlon. Giving in to overwhelming popular demand. Just to liven things up, you

155

know? Save us all from the end-of-summer blues?"

"You took action on the triathlon?" Ben's voice was a leaden mix of incredulity and fury.

"Sophisticate up, will you, guy?" Winston returned. "Gambling's the, um, innocent something of an illicit pleasure. It's the original crimeless victim. I mean, victimless crime. In an enlightened society—"

"Stop!" Ben roared. "Don't give me any more of that nonsense!"

Jessica gaped in wonder and alarm as Ben's cheeks reddened, his eyes seemed to double in size, and his voice rose about three octaves.

This was a Ben Mercer she'd never seen before and frankly hoped never to see again. Was it possible that he was some kind of crazy moralist underneath the easygoing exterior? He'd been nice enough to Winston about having bet everyone's merit pay on the outcome of the triathlon.

"You clown!" Ben hurled at Winston. "How could you have been so stupid? You can't run in a race if you've taken bets on it. Didn't that thought penetrate your pea brain? You remember that baseball player who went to jail for indulging in the same 'innocent pleasure'? That's you, babe. Well, so much for your terrific time on the bike. You're out of the race."

"Out of the race?" Jessica echoed miserably.

"You're not our captain," Winston protested haughtily, but Jessica could see that he was almost in tears.

"You're out of the race," Nina snapped. "Is that official enough for you?"

Jessica knelt down next to Winston. "Oh, leave him alone, you two. Can't you see how terrible he feels?" She hugged him. "I'm sorry, Winnie." She hardly ever used the nickname he'd gotten while living in a girls' dorm. "I know you didn't mean to do anything awful."

"Don't call me Winnie," he said mournfully. "I don't deserve it. Ben's right. I don't know what I was thinking of. Or not thinking of."

"Well, you better start thinking and fast," Ben said crisply. "You better think yourself out of the bookie business ASAP or you're going to find yourself in trouble with the law—not just with us. And the judge won't give a hoot how lovable you are."

Winston eased Nina off his back and turned to face them. "I'm sorry, guys. I really am."

"We know, Winston," Nina said with a little sigh.

"Whatever happens to me, I won't let any of the disgrace touch you guys," Winston said with passion, his voice rising in a lyrical spiral. "No matter what kind of deal they offer to cut me, I won't rat you out. All I ask—"

"Get a grip, Winston," Ben interrupted him. "There's nobody to rat out. We didn't do anything wrong—except trust you."

"I guess you won't make that mistake again." Winston's long face crumpled.

157

"Sure we will," Jessica assured him. She flashed an angry glance at Ben. "Again and again and again."

Nina needed to work off some tension. Her shoulders felt as stiff as Winston's had a little while ago. She could use a massage, a professional one, but she couldn't afford it—especially not now. Well, there was always the Beach Bum, where for a couple of quarters she could take out her frustrations on one of the world's all-time greatest pinball machines.

Nina knew the Beach Bum would be dark inside, even in the middle of the day. She liked it there because of the fresh fruit smoothies the bartender whipped up to please his underage crowd and because it had a vintage pinball machine with gorgeously sensitive flippers and a very forgiving tilt mechanism.

Her spirits lifted as she detected the glow of the machine against the far wall. She made a beeline for it, her eyes slowly adjusting to the dim room.

In the shadows it took a moment for her to recognize the tall guy who was racking up points off the top bumpers as he deftly leaned into the machine and gave it a subtle shake.

But he must have caught her reflection in the polished glass because he recognized her without turning around.

"Two-player game?" he challenged.

She recognized the mellow voice and detected the faint scent of lime.

"No, thanks," she said coldly.

"Come on, wouldn't it be good for us to have a little friendly competition before we get into the serious stuff this weekend?"

"I'd rather not."

Paul turned around to face her. "Wow, we are one competitive female, aren't we?" Shaking his head, he flashed his ten-thousand-kilowatt smile. "You really don't know what you're missing," he added, making it clear that he was talking about more than pinball.

Nina was suddenly very aware that her striped spandex leotard emphasized every nuance of her figure. She wished she'd bothered to pull on a sweatshirt. Well, she would just have to clothe herself in words.

"I happen to be as proud of being a female as I'm proud of being of color, and I'll thank you not to use the word as an epithet," she declared with a haughty toss of her braids. "My refusal to play with you has nothing to do with gender. Or with competitiveness either."

As usual the more fiery she got, the more visibly Paul relaxed. His smile grew improbably wider and brighter.

"Oh, yeah? Then what's it about?" he tossed back easily.

"It's about what you are," Nina said. "A thief."

The word seemed to echo in the air, then a

stillness descended between them. The background sounds of the bar—the laughter, the curses, the scraping barstools and whirring blender—grew abruptly louder, as though someone had turned up the volume.

"So what did I steal, your heart?" Paul asked. His voice had the old light mockery, but she was certain that he was maintaining his smile only with effort.

"You know what you stole," she said. "And so does Captain Feehan. It seems that every time I turn around, he's looking for you."

"Paul the ever popular," he murmured. For a moment he looked frankly unhappy, but then the mood seemed to pass.

"Hey, listen, I've got three free games on the machine, won by these talented hands," he said to Nina. "Allow me to bequeath them to you. Perhaps they'll compensate in some small way for whatever I've stolen from you."

Before she could say a word, he vanished into the crowd.

Jessica couldn't stop crying. Reality had sunk in, and she couldn't stop thinking that any minute she and Ben would have to say good-bye—possibly forever. On top of that her foot was throbbing and itching beneath its bandage, and she was terrified that her wound was infected.

She tried to cheer herself up by focusing her thoughts on the cute doctor who'd stitched her wound and then dressed it. The trouble was, she didn't want him. She didn't want anybody but Ben.

She went on sobbing into her pillow until she was drained of tears. Then she sat up and blew her nose.

There's no way around it, she decided. *I'll just have to do everything I can to make sure that Sweet Valley wins the triathlon—no matter what.*

Wendy and Paloma Perro were on dog patrol. A lifeguard didn't need a dog on a leash in order to enforce the rule against dogs not on leashes, but Wendy found that it helped to have a canine partner. Other dog owners couldn't accuse her of being an animal hater. And Paloma looked so perpetually content, even when fettered, that he was a kind of living advertisement for the joys of the leash.

Wendy knew that she, on the other hand, was hardly an advertisement for the joys of anything. She couldn't stop thinking about the latest incident with Rachel, and the more she thought about it, the unhappier she got.

Rachel was beautiful. Men seemed to find her hard to resist, though Wendy was darned if she could see why.

Wendy couldn't help picturing Pedro and Rachel together. She scanned the beach, almost hoping for an illegally liberated pooch or some other infraction or minor disaster to distract her.

But this seemed to be the day for peaceful family picnics on neatly spread-out blankets. No one even had a radio turned up to a level that might bother somebody else. The most exciting diversion of the afternoon was Paloma's noisy insistence that one family's bucket of fried chicken had his name on it.

The Rachel and Pedro movie played on in Wendy's mind. They were lounging by the pool, her lustrous dark head on his thigh as he strummed his guitar. His earring flashed in the sunlight, or was it the moonlight? No, wait a minute, edit that—Rachel couldn't rest her head on his right thigh; that was where the guitar perched. On his left thigh, then—but, oh, what did the details matter? The point was that the basic picture made sense. They'd look perfect together.

Rachel and Pedro. Laughing about how he'd tricked Wendy into looking after Carlos and the house while he was gone. Of course he could easily have afforded to hire a caretaker, Wendy imagined him explaining as he strummed heart-tugging chords, but some kinds of loyalty you could buy more easily with promises of love than with money.

The funny thing was, Wendy almost felt sorry for Pedro. The conceited singer didn't know that Rachel was interested in things, not human beings. He might not yet be a household name, but Pedro was definitely making more money than anyone else at Sweet Valley Shore—more than all the lifeguards put together, and then some. Rachel was using him, the way she'd used Ben, the way Winston said she was using Harry.

Wendy sat down for a moment in front of one of the jetties that served as a natural line of demarcation between the beaches. Burying her head in Paloma's shaggy coat, she began to cry.

A shout cut into her pity party.

"Help! Somebody save me! I'm drowning! Help!"

Wendy's tears seemed to freeze on her cheeks.

"Stay!" she ordered Paloma. Blowing twice on her whistle to alert the other guards, she ran into the surf.

The water had never felt so cold. Her muscles contracted abruptly, but she ran through the pain and didn't falter. She went on running until she reached her depth, then made a shallow racing dive in the direction of the guy whose flailing arms were her beacon.

She angled through the waves at breakneck speed, spurred on by the dreaded words.

Help! I'm drowning! Help!

He was tall and big, about two hundred muscular pounds of blond teenager, and she was awfully glad he didn't struggle. In fact, he was as cooperative a drowning victim as she'd ever rescued—unless you counted the "drowning" Pedro had staged to lure her to his side. As she got him in her grasp and began to make for shore, she could feel him rhythmically kicking his feet.

When they got to the beach, she collapsed, exhausted by the effort and the tension. "You OK?" she gasped.

"Yeah, I'm fine. Thanks. Thanks a lot," he added. "That was a close one."

Wendy's eyes narrowed. This guy was either the calmest, coolest character she'd ever met or something else was going on here.

"Did you ever have an incident like this before?" she asked. "You seem like a pretty good swimmer."

The kid shook his head. "I just had a panic attack or something. I mean, I got stomach cramps." He bent over, clutching his middle, by way of illustration. "And then I thought I saw a shark."

"A shark! There are no sharks in these waters."

"Well, whatever it was, I didn't want to be alone with it. See you around." With a little wave he started off.

"Wait!" Wendy called. "I have to file a report. What's your name?"

"Joe."

"Joe what?" Wendy asked.

"Joe Smith, do you believe it?"

"No, actually, I don't," Wendy muttered to herself as she and Paloma jogged back toward the lifeguard station for an incident sheet.

When she went to the desk, she realized instantly

what had happened. *Oh, you fool, Wendy!*

The shark had been plying the land, not the water.

While she'd been busily "rescuing" the so-called Joe Smith, someone had broken into the locked drawer again. All eyes had been on her rescue. Even the lifeguards sitting at the station hadn't noticed the intruder.

What nerve!

This time she had not only lost her cash, she'd lost her wallet. And the keys to Pedro's house as well!

All summer Elizabeth had meant to visit Tilton's famous mission-style church. But she hadn't expected to find herself across the street from the pink stucco structure today.

She rubbed her disbelieving eyes as she watched Ryan and the red-haired woman meet in front of the church. They hugged, clasped hands, and strolled on in together.

What on earth could it mean? Why would a man and woman, both in jeans, visit a church on a weekday?

Ryan didn't strike her as an architecture buff. So maybe . . . maybe . . . he was signing on to teach a Sunday school class?

Except that in his passionate words about the almighty ocean, he'd never indicated any conventional religious beliefs. Certainly not enough to merit teaching sacred studies.

And then it hit her. The single possibility that made real sense.

"No," she moaned softly. "Please. No."

But all the pleading in the world wasn't going to change the truth.

A man and a woman in casual clothes who walked into a church on a weekday could be there for only one reason.

They were planning their wedding!

Chapter Ten

Elizabeth peered down the empty hallway. The closed doors offered no enlightenment beyond their nameplates. *Seth Janifer—Associate Pastor. Charles Knipe, Choirmaster.* One door, decorated with smiley faces bearing first names, clearly led to a Sunday school classroom, as a peek through the window confirmed. The air smelled thick and un-stirred, and she got the distinct feeling that the of-fices behind the nameplates were deserted.

Finally she saw a man coming toward her. "Can I help you?" he asked in a friendly voice.

Elizabeth opened her mouth, but she didn't know what to say. How could she possibly explain her mission?

The man offered a comforting smile, conveying the impression that he knew exactly what she was going through.

"Don't be embarrassed," he said. "We've all

been in your shoes. It's in the basement. Come on, I'll go with you."

She was too confused to protest, and the next thing she knew, the man was opening the door to a big room . . . *full of people!*

Elizabeth blinked.

She looked at the assorted men and women sitting on folding chairs, clutching paper cups of coffee. A political meeting of some sort? And where were Ryan and the redhead?

And then she saw him. He was on his way to the podium at the front of the room. The redhead was looking up at him, her hands clasped prayerfully and her eyes brimming with pride.

He clutched the podium and cleared his throat, then cleared it again.

"My name is Ryan," he said. The words came out a bare whisper.

"My name is Ryan," he said again, this time almost shouting. He looked helplessly at the red-haired woman.

Members of the audience smiled encouragingly. One or two began to clap softly and rhythmically. A man in a wheelchair raised his coffee cup in a silent toast.

Ryan grasped the podium with both hands and looked straight ahead. When he spoke, his voice was at a normal pitch, and the words flowed easily.

"My name is Ryan and I'm an alcoholic."

Winston's fingers trembled as he tore open

the wrapping paper on the package postmarked Marseilles. Without a doubt, this was the last present he was going to receive from Denise. When school started and she heard what a moron he'd been, how he'd put the whole Sweet Valley gang at risk every which way—it was going to be "*Adieu,* Winston. Good-bye."

He vowed then and there never to tell her that it had all been for her. Because really it hadn't been all for her, had it? If he looked way down deep into his murky soul, he had to admit that he liked breaking the rules and doing things backward. As his weirdly indulgent science teacher had once put it, he was one of those types who seemed determined to prove that the laws of gravity didn't apply to him. Which meant, his teacher had added cheerfully, that he was probably going to end up winning the Nobel Prize or spending half his life in jail.

He unwrapped the package and held up the contents. It was an authentic blue-and-white French fisherman's jersey.

I always said you'd look cute in stripes, the card read. Beaucoup *love, Denise.*

Winston pictured himself in convict stripes. How long did a first-time bookie get in jail?

He began to laugh hysterically. Was Denise's present a loving coincidence . . . or a prophetic glimpse of dire things to come?

Elizabeth sat spellbound as Ryan spoke.

He was visibly nervous, with rings of perspiration apparent on his shirtsleeves, yet he had never looked handsomer or more imposing. As he revealed his story, unpeeling layer by layer of his secret struggle, the guarded expression on his face gave way to a contagious serenity.

"Like everyone else in this room, I thought that I was the master and alcohol was the slave," Ryan said. "Boy, was I deluded—or do I mean diluted?"

Several people laughed encouragingly, and Ryan went on.

"My other delusion was that I only drank beer, so it didn't really count. The worst part was the calories. I kept telling myself that since I worked out, I'd keep burning off the calories. So that took care of that little problem."

Pausing, he took a sip of water and looked at the red-haired woman. "Well, no, there was an even more dangerous delusion. You see, I thought that drinking was only about the night before. I didn't know that it was also about the morning after. One morning last summer I didn't go to work because I was too hung over. One of my rookies took over, and, well, it was the end of the world. A little girl drowned." His voice caught and he drew a ragged breath. "She died."

He wiped sweat from his forehead. From somewhere in the audience Elizabeth heard a sob.

She sank back into her chair, stunned. So *that* was why Ryan was so hard on himself about the accident the previous summer.

"Nothing can bring her back." Ryan's voice was trembling. "I think about her every single day. When I see other kids her age, I go crazy. The police captain down at the beach says no one could have saved her. She tumbled out of a sailboat, way offshore, and she was wearing the wrong kind of life preserver, so she didn't stay faceup. Maybe it's arrogant of me to think I could have saved her, but I know I would have had the best shot at it."

"Ryan," Elizabeth whispered. "My poor Ryan."

"Anyway, that's about it," Ryan continued. "The day of the drowning I wanted to go off on the biggest bender of all time, but Captain Feehan persuaded me to come here instead. I fell off the wagon once, but then I got back on. As of today I am one year sober."

The red-haired woman got up, and Ryan smiled at her. "I want to thank Patti, everyone in the program, and Captain Feehan. I'd especially like to thank a woman who isn't here but who helped me more than she'll ever know. And thank You, above all," he murmured, raising his eyes heavenward.

Patti shook his hand and kissed him on the cheek as everyone applauded.

"Thank you, Ryan, for that beautiful sharing. I'm proud to present you with this certificate of one year's sobriety."

As the applause grew louder Elizabeth got to her feet, clapping with an echoing fervor.

Suddenly Ryan's face grew pale.

171

He'd seen her, and he muttered something briefly to Patti.

Slowly Elizabeth walked toward Ryan. Their eyes met and locked in a tumultuous gaze.

Ryan's eyes were fearful, but Elizabeth didn't waver. She could almost feel the ferocity in her own expression.

"Do you hate me?" Ryan whispered.

"Hate you?" Elizabeth shook her head vehemently. "Never. I don't think I've ever been as proud of anybody else in my whole life."

She put her arms around him. She longed to tell him that the drowning hadn't been his fault; no one could have saved that child. He was only a man—not a superhero, but she knew it wasn't the time for such words.

Someday, maybe, he would find a way of forgiving himself. Meanwhile the most important thing was to let him know how deeply she approved of the step he had taken to free himself from alcohol's grip on his life.

"You are the most courageous man I know . . . to stand up there like that," she said.

He shrugged. "Everyone does it, sooner or later."

"But not with such grace, I bet," she declared loyally. Smiling shyly, she added, "Will you introduce me to Patti?" The other woman had tactfully moved out of earshot when Elizabeth had approached Ryan.

The old panicky look crossed his face again,

then he seemed to realize he had nothing to hide, nothing to lose.

"Why not?" He took her by the hand.

"Elizabeth, this is Patti. Patti, meet Elizabeth."

The two women shook hands and exchanged undisguised looks of interest. Patti looked older than Elizabeth had first thought her to be, but she was undeniably attractive. Just because she had a kind of professional relationship with Ryan didn't mean that was the end of the story.

"So you're Elizabeth," Patti said warmly. "I'm pleased to know you. Ryan says you've been very helpful to him."

Elizabeth reeled. "I think you must have me confused with someone else. Today is the first I even knew that Ryan had a problem with alcohol."

"People sometimes help without knowing it," Patti said softly. "Maybe I'll leave you two to discuss this. Help yourself to coffee, Elizabeth. And the cookies are homemade—you must try one. The chocolate chip are especially good."

"Recovering alcoholics tend to like sweet stuff," Ryan explained, leading Elizabeth to the refreshment table.

Wow, Elizabeth thought as she bit into a cookie. Would anyone believe this? Did she believe it herself? All those weeks of sizzling tension, all the should-I-or-shouldn't-I debates with herself, all the heartbreak and all the glorious kissing—and now here she and Ryan were, chatting away as relaxed as could be, as if they were old friends hanging out in one of the campus coffee shops.

"You seem transformed," she commented as he affably accepted the congratulatory handshakes of some of his fellow members. "I can't remember the last time I saw you this relaxed."

"Well, I've been dreading today. I didn't know whether I'd have the nerve to go through with it. I really wanted that certificate, but I wanted a beer even more."

"After a year you still want one?" she asked, amazed.

"I'll always want one," he returned easily. "There isn't a person in this room who doesn't want a drink right now—except for you. That's why we have to keep coming back. That's why there's so much emphasis on one day at a time."

"Phew." Elizabeth let out a huge sigh. "Have I learned a lot today."

Suddenly the crowd broke into a raucous rendition of "Happy Birthday."

Elizabeth smiled and automatically joined in. "What name?" she asked Ryan, who wasn't singing.

"It's for me," he whispered bashfully. "Because the day you opt for sobriety is like a rebirth."

With tears in her eyes Elizabeth sang the words "dear Ryan." She knew she would never again hear the birthday song without remembering this moment.

As people started moving toward the door a

silence fell between Elizabeth and Ryan. She knew what she had to do.

"I bet you and Patti have plans for dinner or something," she said easily. "And I have to head home. Believe it or not, I didn't sleep a wink last night."

"Why not?" Ryan asked.

"It's a long story. Anyway, I want to get on the road while I'm still alert."

"Thanks for being doubly understanding," Ryan said. "You're right, Patti's bringing me home for dinner. Her husband's the chef at the Trail's End Pub, but tonight's his night off."

Elizabeth felt a surge of relief at the word *husband*.

"Isn't it hard on you, working in a bar?" she asked to cover her emotions.

"Everyone discouraged me at first, but I felt it was no good pretending the temptation wasn't there. And since Patti's also a recovering alcoholic, at least I have someone I can run to if things start to get out of control."

Yes, that was Ryan, all right, Elizabeth thought. The man of iron, eternally testing himself.

Elizabeth paused at the doorway to read a poster displaying the famous twelve steps of Alcoholics Anonymous.

She pointed to number eight, about making amends to people harmed in the past.

Ryan's fists clenched. "That's the one I can never fulfill. How do you make amends to an angel in heaven?" His eyes watered.

"Maybe you should concentrate on a few people still on earth," Elizabeth said seriously. She laid a tender hand on his arm. "I know it's not remotely the same thing, but I can think of a whole bunch of people whose lives you made harder by cutting out this summer. Nina, Captain Feehan . . . our whole squad. And meanwhile you made life a little better for Rachel and the South Beach gang," she couldn't resist adding.

"I did do that, didn't I?" Ryan said. "Would it help if I said I'm dreadfully sorry?"

A part of Elizabeth wanted to let him off the hook after all he'd been through, but another part of her resisted.

"I'm afraid it's going to take more than words," she told him.

She kissed him on the cheek—the most innocent of kisses—but it was all she could do to pull herself out of his magnetic proximity and thrust herself toward the Jeep.

As she drove through the lengthening shadows an unnerving thought occurred to her. Ryan had the same effect on her that beer had on him. He was a seductive but lethal intoxicant that she was never going to stop wanting, no matter how long she stayed sober.

Was there a Lovers Anonymous to take her in and help her through the rough spots? Because she wasn't at all sure she could make it alone.

Chapter
Eleven

The others had gone to the movies after dinner, but Elizabeth had known she wouldn't be able to concentrate.

Her head was full of Ryan. His pain. His courage. The tangled emotions between them.

His revelations in the church basement had explained a great deal. But not everything.

Because she still loved Tom.

She felt a little bit as if she were defying gravity. It was supposed to be impossible. You couldn't really love two guys—love them from way deep down—this much.

But she did.

She knew that she would go back to Tom at the end of the summer, but that didn't stop her from looking out her bedroom window at the profusion of stars. And making a wish on one of them.

Let him come back. Let Ryan come home to all of

us. I know I can't have him always and forever, but I can have that much.

One of the stars seemed to wink at her. And then grow impossibly bright.

But it wasn't a star. It was the light in the lifeguard station.

A fluttery sensation filled her chest.

Her impossible wish had been granted.

Ryan had come home.

Winston offered Wendy their shared popcorn, but she waved it away.

"Look at that ponytail," Wendy whispered, pointing at the movie screen. "Just like Pedro's." She began to sob. "I have to get out of here."

They were sitting in the second row of the theater, one of their many bonds being that they both liked watching movies very close up. Winston instantly reached for his jacket.

"I'll go with you," he said. "I'm just too restless to sit still."

They walked in silence for a while, their clasped hands swinging easily between them as they meandered along the beach toward home.

"I love hanging out with you, Wendy," Winston burst out. "Promise you'll come meet Denise this fall?"

Wendy said she promised.

"And if Pedro really is two-timing you, which I still refuse to believe, I will personally find you his successor." Suddenly Winston put his fingers

178

to his lips. "Do you see what I see?"

"Oh, wow. You mean the light in the lifeguard station?"

"Exactly. Wendy, I think our burglar has returned to the scene of the crime!"

"Would he put on a light that way?" Wendy asked doubtfully.

"Since the beach is closed at night, he probably figures he doesn't have to worry about getting caught. Maybe he's searching for something we never even thought about."

"What, there's gold buried beneath the floorboards?"

"Hey, this is no time to get skeptical on me," Winston said. "You run and get Captain Feehan. I'm going to make sure the fiend doesn't get away." Wendy didn't move, and he gave her a little push. "Come on, what are you waiting for? I'm doing this for you. You're the one who's been robbed twice. And it's my chance to be a hero. Get back in everyone's good graces."

"Winston, every time you try to be a hero—"

"Go!" he cried, and set off down the beach as fast as his legs would carry him.

Nina was sitting next to Ben in an aisle seat, a luxury she only got to enjoy when she wasn't with the longer-legged Bryan. She was surprised that Ben came to the movies since Jessica decided not to join everyone. Apparently her foot was still bothering her.

"I thought it was a great idea to come to the movies, but I think it would do more good to be practicing," he said.

Nina reluctantly peeled her eyes from the screen. "At night?"

"We could run."

"You know, I still think we're going to have to forfeit," Nina said. "Barring the miracle that looks extremely unlikely to happen."

"Shhh. Shhh. Shhh!" came from every corner of the theater.

"We can't give up," Ben said desperately. "They may have the leg power, but we have the brains. We'll think of something. Meanwhile let's move those legs."

The manager was tying up thick green plastic garbage bags when Ben and Nina strode past him in the lobby. His eyes widened. "Is something wrong?" he asked.

"Nope," Ben said. "But could we have your garbage bags?"

"Huh?" he said.

"Huh?" Nina said.

"We need to practice running with weights," Ben explained. "Slinging a bag apiece over our shoulder will be just the thing."

"If you promise to dispose of them properly," the manager said in a doubtful voice.

"We are very good friends of the environment," Ben averred solemnly. "You can ask Captain Feehan if you have any doubt."

"Captain Feehan! Oh, that won't be necessary," the man said hurriedly. "Take all the garbage you want!"

"Elizabeth."
"Ryan."

Elizabeth drank in the sight of him in his plain white T-shirt and faded jeans. She hadn't bothered to change out of jeans and a soft teal top that was like a sweatshirt with short sleeves that she'd been wearing when she'd seen him earlier that day in Tilton.

She set down the wicker basket she was carrying. She felt his eyes on her, and she knew that her face and body were all he needed to see. She'd been right not to change—her clothes or anything else.

His lips touched hers briefly. His hands remained at his sides, as though he didn't trust himself to hold her.

Then he was clasping her close to him, and her hands were on his arms, around his back, reaching up to touch his hair. Their lips pressed into each other, and Elizabeth's mouth seemed to be made up of a million nerve endings, each one alive as it had never been before.

He broke the clinch, but with an air of reluctance, softly kissing her eyelids.

Moths fluttered against the window screens, creating an eerie music. The smell of salt filled Elizabeth's nostrils.

The very essence of summer love seemed distilled into that moment. Its heady feeling of total freedom. Its fleeting sweetness.

"I brought you a few things," she murmured. "Milk. Some French bread. There's coffee in the fridge."

"Thanks," he said. He shook his head with a funny little smile. "You know me well. I didn't stop for provisions. For anything."

He put the milk in the refrigerator, then came back to her. "Were you ever here at night before?" Ryan asked.

"No." She set her basket down on the stenciled tea crate that served as a coffee table.

"It's when I like it the best," Ryan said. "You know what I really love to do? Turn off the lights and climb up into the chair."

"Can you see anything?"

"Oh, it's amazing what you can see. There are phosphorescent creatures you can't spot from eye level. And you're a bit closer to heaven." He swung her into his arms. "Of course having you here has the same effect."

His mouth closed over hers in another dizzying kiss.

When she could speak again, she asked the question she had to have answered. "What if I hadn't come to you tonight? Would you have come to me?"

He held her silently. "I have to be honest," he said. "I came back for all of you. Patti told me you

182

were right—that I had to make amends with Nina and the rest of the squad. I came here to put on my whistle again and race in the triathlon, and if I got to do nothing else, that would still feel pretty good. When you tapped at the door tonight, it was like a prayer answered—but a prayer from so deep in my heart I hadn't even dared to know it was there. Because you know I have no right to want you."

"You do," she said fiercely.

He sighed. "Love is easy, Elizabeth. It's commitment that's the tough one."

"But you do want me?"

"Oh, Liz, do you doubt it? You were the woman I talked about when I did my sharing, do you realize that? Yes, I want you. I wish so much that I were nineteen and nothing else mattered but us. I'm just so afraid of letting you down. I couldn't stand to hurt you."

"Let's turn out the lights," she suggested softly. "Let's go up and sit in the chair and see what the stars tell us."

He pulled the chain on the overhead light while she switched off the single lamp.

A moment later the door flew open.

"Freeze or I'll shoot!" a voice cut through the darkness.

Nina and Ben were running along the deserted beach when Nina heard Winston's shout.

"We've got to go help Winston! Move it!"

"I thought you were furious at him," Ben said through ragged breaths.

"What does that have to do with anything? Come on! Move it!"

"If we drop the garbage, we'll run faster," Ben pointed out.

"No, it might make a great weapon—who knows what we're up against? Come on!"

"Winston, are you crazy?" Elizabeth cried, pulling open the door of the lifeguard station.

"Elizabeth!" he gasped. "Ryan! What are you doing here?"

"No, Winston," Ryan said through compressed lips. "I think the question is, what are *you* doing here?"

"I, um, er—" he began.

"Right, Winston." Elizabeth put her hands on her hips. "There it is, the story of your life in a nutshell."

"I feel like a total idiot," Winston mumbled. "I'll just slink off now and let you two get back to whatever you were doing."

Ryan held up his hand. "Please, not another word," he said. "Quit while you're behind. See you in the morning," he added in a kinder voice.

Winston gaped. "You mean you're back?"

"Looks like it, doesn't it?" Ryan returned.

Winston grinned until Elizabeth feared his face would split. He threw his arms around Ryan and smacked kisses onto both his cheeks. "I love

184

you! I'll never be scared of you again."

Ryan's mouth twisted. "I wish I could say as much."

Elizabeth shut the door behind Winston. Almost immediately she heard a series of loud thumps followed by a scream. She yanked the door open and ran outside.

Winston was lying on the ground covered with a mound of popcorn, paper cups, and candy wrappers.

Elizabeth broke into gales of laughter. All the doubting and questioning and agonizing and misunderstanding of the summer seemed to burst out of her with a cleansing roar.

She heard Ryan laugh as she'd never heard him before. Nina and Ben had collapsed onto the sand in laughter. Wendy started to dig Winston out from under the garbage, then gave up in a fit of helpless giggles.

But Winston laughed loudest of all. "We're going to win!" he shouted between peals. "Ryan's back, and we're going to win!"

Chapter
Twelve

Wendy hastily scrawled postcards to the people she hadn't gotten around to writing to all summer—Aunt Charlotte and her ex-roommate, Lucy, now married to an actual titled Englishman and living in London.

She'd thought she had all the time in the world. Only minutes ago, it seemed, summer had stretched before her, as endless as the ocean.

Now it was Saturday of Labor Day weekend. She visualized herself back in Nevada, unpacking, shedding tears of nostalgia as the scent of sea and sun rose up at her. She didn't like the picture.

This summer was supposed to last forever—the Pedro part, anyway. Not a summer like all other summers.

Picture-perfect weather, she wrote on her cards—true. *Happy as can be,* she penned—not true.

She tried to focus on the positive. Ryan was back. Sweet Valley Shore would win the triathlon. Winston would be OK with his friends.

But what good was it to win a race if you lost in love?

If Pedro hadn't gotten in touch by now, he wasn't going to—except to claim his keys, which she'd lost as well.

She pulled her straight hair back into a ponytail and slathered on sunblock. She was wearing her official red swimsuit with her red lifeguard T-shirt over it. Normally you only got to wear lifeguard togs when you were on duty, but Captain Feehan had made an exception for the triathlon.

As she headed to the lifeguard station for the rally Ryan had called, she was amazed at the size of the crowd. Townsfolk and summer people had turned out for the triathlon as if it were the World Series and Rose Bowl combined.

Wendy spotted Pedro's next-door neighbors, Pedro's dog groomer, Pedro's gardener (with his son perched on his shoulders). She traded waves with the owner of the Sand Bar, where Wendy first saw Pedro perform live.

Only Pedro himself was missing.

The rest of the lifeguards were already at the station and everyone looked psyched. Jessica had improvised a cheerleader's outfit, complete with pompoms from the local five-and-ten. Winston's eyes were flashing dollar signs again. Nina was vibrating with the need to leave Paul in the dust, while

Elizabeth and Ryan shimmered with their desire to come through for each other.

Ryan blew his whistle, and everyone stopped talking.

"Listen up, people—" he began.

No sooner had he gotten the three familiar words out than a tumultuous cheer rose from the eight lifeguards in front of him. No one had called them "people" in that crisp voice since the day he'd left, and their applause made it clear how much they'd missed the commanding sound.

Wendy had had her differences with him, but she clapped until her hands ached. Along with the others she called his name, repeatedly and rhythmically.

"Ryan, Ryan—"

"Thanks," he said simply, holding up his hand. "But this is about all of us. This is about being a team."

"Yay, team!" Jessica shouted, waving her pompoms.

Ryan shushed her with a look—not stern, but not kidding around either.

"Let's start with the basics," he said. "I want you all to put on your bike helmets so I can check the fit. Did everyone bring a water bottle?" He scanned the group. "Good. Now check out your running shoes. Everyone's laces the right length? The last thing we need is to get tripped up by something dopey."

Paula decided that her laces were too long, and

he miraculously found a spare pair to fit her.

"OK," Ryan went on when everyone was ready to listen again. "I'm not going to give you any bull this morning," he rapped out. "It's going to be close. We have no margin for error here. Come on, Wendy, reeeeeeach for that ankle. Where are your leg warmers, Marcus? I told you I wanted leg warmers. We can't afford any cramped muscles."

"They make my legs look fat," Marcus quipped.

"Hey, you sound like me," Jessica said.

Wendy felt a lump form in her throat. She was going to miss this crazy crowd. They'd gotten so familiar with one another. They had in-jokes that couldn't possibly be translated for outsiders. A kind of secret code.

Mostly, though, she would miss Pedro—or the idea of Pedro. It had been beautiful before the bubble burst.

If Pedro were here, I could fly like the wind, Wendy thought. *Swim like a shark. And bike a hundred miles, not just ten.* But he wasn't there, and her feet felt as heavy as her heart.

No, she mustn't think that way. She had to think victory.

Winston gave a shout. "Duck, guys! We're being bombed by South Beach!"

A squad of planes was swooping down toward them. For a moment Wendy was frightened, then Jessica exclaimed with delight.

"Look, everyone! It's the sky typists!"

Even Ryan had to stop stretching and focus on the puffy white letters taking shape above them.

"Good luck, Sweet Valley Shore!" Jessica read aloud. "Love, Jenny and Quinn."

"I don't believe it!" Nina said.

"It's a couple that Nina and Elizabeth saved," Jessica explained to Ryan. "The guy behaved like a total idiot. I mean, not only didn't he thank Nina, he yelled at her for not going back for his boat. I guess this is his way of saying he's sorry."

"Men are weird about being saved." Ryan's meaningful glance at Elizabeth wasn't lost on Wendy. Would anyone ever look at her that way again?

Come back to me, Pedro. Come back to the girl with the smoke-colored eyes.

"Well, this time the sky typing's at least partly for you," Ben said to Jessica.

"Oh, who cares about what's in the sky as long as I have you on the ground?" Jessica replied dreamily.

Wendy was glad that her friends were happy, but her own unhappiness only loomed the blacker.

She made up her mind. She would give her all to her teammates, but as soon as the race was over, she was packing up and shipping out. She wouldn't wait for the weekend to end. She'd just slip off. Winston would take care of Carlos, Jessica would adopt Paloma, and Wendy would put Sweet Valley Shore behind her forever.

* * *

190

"Can everyone hear me?" Captain Feehan roared through his bullhorn.

"Yes!" the crowd roared back.

"Is it a great day for our annual triathlon or what?" came the booming words.

"Yeah!" came the reply.

"I'd like to thank the following civic-minded merchants and citizens for donating goods, services, and this bea-u-ti-ful weather. Harry's Hamburgers and Hot Dog Howie's, Fox Printing, the Beach Bum, the Abrahms Insurance Agency, the Sand Bar, Katie Stern Catering, the—"

Any minute he was going to thank his mother and his first-grade teacher, Elizabeth thought impatiently. Some people should never be allowed to get their hands on a bullhorn.

"And my mother, who encouraged me to pursue a career in law enforcement. Also my first-grade teacher, Mrs. Emma Jane Walls, who taught me that it was no disgrace to want to win as long as you fought fair."

As Captain Feehan paused for breath the crowd began stomping and clapping. "We want action. We want action."

"What?" Captain Feehan teased.

"Action, action, action," chanted the crowd.

"Louder!" Captain Feehan screamed. Elizabeth thought she might explode.

"Will the opposing captains, Rachel Max and Ryan Taylor, please come forward and shake hands?"

As the handshake took place to tumultuous cheers (and a few boos that were quickly silenced), Captain Feehan directed the participants to put on their helmets. The first event would be the ten-mile bicycle race, three and a half laps around the greensward. A half-mile swim would follow, and the meet would conclude with a mile-long run in full scuba gear, minus flippers.

The starting pistol cracked. Elizabeth felt as if she'd been shot into the air.

The crowd disappeared. There was nothing in the world but Elizabeth and her bike. As she arched over the handlebars, she had the glorious illusion that if she kept pumping hard enough, her wheels wouldn't touch the ground until she flew across the finish line.

She was dimly aware that the silvery blur in the lead was Ryan. She and Ben were maybe a hundred meters behind, neck and neck with the two best cyclists on the South Beach squad, Tina and Kyle.

Elizabeth's heart was pounding like crazy, but it was a wonderful pounding—an exhilarating mix of love, energy, will, and sheer joy in being alive.

Sweat poured down her face, and for the briefest of seconds she took her left hand off the handlebar to wipe it away. At that moment Tina and Kyle split to surround her and Ben.

In the same instant the South Beach cyclists reached out and shoved her and Ben, knocking them off balance and into each other.

Elizabeth screamed. Trying to regain her equilibrium, she careened into Ben and they both flew off their bikes.

Fighting back tears of rage, Elizabeth checked to make sure that Ben was unhurt. Then, without wasting a moment, she scrambled back onto her bike.

"We're all right, keep going," she shouted ahead to Ryan. But he had paused and waited until he was sure that they were steadily on course, pedaling for all they were worth.

Rachel zoomed past the three of them, but Elizabeth was flabbergasted at her behavior. Rachel was yelling at her own teammates as she drew abreast of them.

"Play fair or I'm conceding the race!" she berated them.

Elizabeth could hardly believe her ears. Rachel suddenly hung up on sportsmanship?

"No dirty tricks. Understand?" Rachel screamed. She reached out, and for a crazy second it looked to Elizabeth as if Rachel were going to topple Tina.

What in the world was going on?

Winston and Jessica tried to console each other. South Beach had won the cycling, but Sweet Valley had the swimmers. With any luck they'd be all even after the next heat. And then maybe, maybe—

Jessica put her face in her hands. "Who are we

kidding, Winston? Ryan may be practically an Olympic swimmer, but a runner he's not. Have you ever seen Janet or Paul run? Their feet don't touch the ground."

"You're better than them," Winston declared loyally.

"Yeah, I admit I'm pretty fast, but what difference does it make? I'm not running." Jessica disconsolately swung her bandaged foot. "Foot, I hate you!" she shouted in frustration. "No, I don't," she crooned a minute later as her foot retaliated with an itching attack. "It's not your fault, foot. It's that stupid knife's fault."

"You mean the fault of whoever dropped the knife," Winston said.

"Yeah. Mr. Paul Whoever. The alleged Mr. Paul Whoever, I guess I should say. Innocent until proven guilty and all that, but do you know how my foot craves to get even by proving him guilty right in the shinbone?"

"Ouch." Winston rubbed his leg as if he, not Paul, had received the theoretical kick. "Well, I'd better get back to work." He was back in hamburger regalia, walking the boardwalk in hope of wowing the holiday tourists.

"That's the only work you're doing now for Harry, isn't it, Winston?" Jessica asked sternly.

"You sound like Ben," Winston said. "I hope you don't start to look like him too. I definitely prefer you with long blond hair."

Jessica frowned. "Seriously, Winston."

"Yeah, yeah. I'm out of the bookie business. Harry writes everything down now."

"While you innocently look on?" Jessica asked in an anxious voice.

"No, I cover my eyes," Winston said. "Really, if we haven't gotten busted by now, I think we're OK. And after today we're both retiring. Harry says he's going straight."

"You mean Hamburger Harry suddenly grew a conscience?"

"Well, even for him it's been a bit of a strain to take money off a kid—though the kid did insist. Boy, that kid must be sweating bullets. He backed Sweet Valley in a really big way. I wish I didn't have this horrible feeling that he was about to learn a very expensive lesson."

"I wish I didn't have a horrible feeling that we're all about to learn an expensive lesson." Jessica sighed.

Limply waving her cheerleader's pompoms, she followed Winston down the boardwalk. *This can't be happening,* she thought. *I can't be losing everything I've worked so hard for all summer. I can't be losing Ben.*

Nina's heart was pounding from exertion and anxiety as Captain Feehan climbed into the lifeguard chair to announce the results of the swimming heat.

"Hear ye, hear ye," he boomed. "Sweet Valley wins the swim competition with an average time of seven minutes, thirty-six seconds, for the half-mile course."

Nina and Ryan threw their arms around each other as Feehan went on to announce that Ryan's time of six minutes, two seconds, had set a new record for the course. Nina had been right behind him with six and a half minutes.

"We did it!" Nina cheered.

"Two, four, six, eight, who do we appreciate!" Jessica cried out in a pompom flurry. "Ryan! Nina! Yay, team!"

Captain Feehan cleared his throat, not a pretty sound when electronically magnified. "Congratulations are also due our fine South Beach swimmers, whose average time of seven minutes, fifty-six seconds, doesn't reflect the outstanding time of Paul and Kristi, who made it across the finish line in seven and a quarter minutes."

"Any minute he's going to start giving the square root of everyone's time," Elizabeth muttered.

"So far, so good," Ryan told his teammates. "But listen up—"

Nina's attention was fixed on Paul, not on Ryan. Paul's back was turned toward her, and beads of water gleamed like diamonds on his dark shoulders. As he shimmied a towel back and forth behind him, his physical grace moved her almost to tears. His character might leave a lot to be desired, but his dark, muscled body was just plain desirable.

As if he felt the heat of her gaze, he suddenly turned—too abruptly for her to be able to avert her eyes. He flashed the famous smile and a congratulatory thumbs-up sign.

Nina was utterly undone, not by his actions but by her own swirl of giddy feelings. If she gave him the teensiest, tinsiest clue, it would be all over for her. He would know his own power at last, and he would move in for the kill.

She mustn't let him know.

Haughtily tilting her nose in the air, she turned resolutely away.

Wendy's breath was coming in jagged gasps. "What sadist dreamed up this costume party?"

"Hey, just be grateful we don't have to breathe through a mouthpiece," Ben managed to say as he loped along next to her. "Or run in flippers!"

Wendy stifled a giggle. She couldn't spare the oxygen. Her normally forgiving lungs were straining under the burden of a wet suit, flotation vest, tank, hoses, and assorted diving equipment.

She tried reminding herself that everyone else, friend and foe, was laboring under the same burden. Indeed, as the sixteen runners trudged along the beach, she thought they looked like a party of aliens whose craft had just touched down at sea.

She resisted the urge to put on a burst of speed and leave the others behind her. Like everyone else, she had to pace herself; the hardest part lay ahead. At the end of the beach stretch was the thickly wooded park they'd bicycled around. This time they had to cut through it, without benefit of trail or tools for bushwhacking. On the far side was the road through the center of town.

When they reached the woods, the pack began to spread out. Wendy and Paul were neck and neck now.

He was a great runner, a long-legged guy who seemed to be composed entirely of muscle, and in other circumstances she would have loved the challenge of being paced by him.

But legs were one thing, and hands were another. She stared at his long fingers and imagined them breaking locks and filching money. She didn't want her neck anywhere near them, least of all on a day when so much was at stake.

Veering away from him, Wendy plunged into the woods on the far side of a small salt pond. Following what seemed to be some sort of path, she suddenly found herself caught up in a tangle of twisted bushes and diving equipment.

A bird screeched. A butterfly winged by her nose, mocking her with its freedom.

She managed to unhook her pressure gauge hose from the branches that had ensnared it, but she'd lost precious minutes.

Worse yet, her sense of direction had deserted her.

She was no longer sure which way she'd come from or which way would take her out of the woods.

Chapter Thirteen

Nina ran through a dreamscape out of her worst nightmares. The ground beneath her feet was eerily soft, a primordial pudding that would suck her in if she didn't keep on moving. But moving was excruciatingly hard. The trees were malevolent creatures, reaching out to snare her. Shrubs seemed to spring up in her path.

For one heart-lifting moment she thought she heard the sounds of civilization—a car horn tooting, a burst of music. Then the woods closed in on her again and all she could hear were the high-pitched sounds of her steamy surroundings.

Her courage faltered. She was tempted to rip off her scuba gear and forfeit the race in order to escape the claustrophobic green. Then she saw Paul in her mind's eye, saw that eternally cocky smile of his. Brandishing a fist, raising her eyes heavenward for courage, she vowed not to quit.

At that moment her foot caught on something directly blocking her path and she went sprawling into the dirt.

She shrieked as she tumbled, instinctively covering her face to keep from being lacerated by brambles. She landed on—

Paul!

For the most horrifying moment of her life, she thought he was dead. Then, incredibly, he winked. Tied up, gagged, and bleeding from a head wound, still he managed to wink.

"One way or another, I knew I'd get you to fall for me," he quipped as her trembling fingers loosened the scarf that had been tied around his mouth.

"What happened?" she cried. "Who did this to you?"

"He didn't stop to introduce himself," Paul said drily. "Jumped me from behind, knocked me out, and then tied me up. I let him think I was unconscious because I wasn't too crazy about the idea of his slugging me again, but I caught a glimpse when he was running away. A kid, I think, couldn't have been more than fourteen or fifteen. Slight kid with dark hair. Round up the usual suspects."

"Oh, Paul," she groaned. "Paul."

"If you get the knife out of my belt and cut the rope around my wrists, I can hold you," he said. "It would feel awfully nice right now."

As Nina took the knife out of its sheath she

suppressed a gasp. It was the same diving knife he'd always had.

But she had to be sure beyond a shadow of a doubt.

"You found your knife?"

He looked puzzled. "Found it? I never lost it."

There was no doubting the sincerity of his words.

Nina could have sobbed with relief. He hadn't dropped it while robbing the lifeguard station!

And that meant he probably hadn't robbed Wendy or been guilty of cutting the rope on the No Swimming sign.

How could she have been so ready to judge him? Was it because it was easier than facing her incredibly powerful attraction for him?

Then anger surged up from deep inside her and pushed aside the guilt.

She had the terrible feeling that she'd been set up. That he—or someone—had *wanted* her to suspect him.

"OK, Paul," she said coolly. "What's the story? What's the real story?"

"Um, Nina? I'm still tied up, for one thing."

For a moment she considered holding him hostage until he told her the truth, but she didn't have the heart. She carefully sliced through the clothesline that bound him.

He ruefully rubbed his chafed wrists, and she winced in sympathy.

"Are you all right?" she asked anxiously.

"Oh, yeah."

"Then tell all," she commanded.

"Nina, it's about this race we're in," he began, sitting up. He brushed twigs off his legs.

She couldn't help noticing that he was as gorgeous when he was dazed and dirty as when he was cool and perfectly polished.

"Oh, yeah, the race," she said. "I wanted to win it more than I've wanted to win anything in a long time—mostly to beat you. You personally, Paul. Because you've made me crazy this summer, in more ways than one. I love my teammates. I wouldn't let them down for anything. But as long as you and I are both out of it, I guess I haven't hurt our average."

"You're being very sporting," he said. He smiled, but the words carried no mockery. "I would have expected nothing less."

"And you're putting off telling me the truth," she said. "Ditto on the expectations." She handed him back his knife and leaned against a mammoth tree trunk, her arms folded across her chest. "Well?"

"OK, it's true. I wanted you to think I was the bad guy. It was a plot that Captain Feehan and I cooked up. I've been working with him to try to catch the real thief, and part of our strategy was to focus suspicion on me. That way the real criminal would get nice and relaxed and maybe screw up enough to get caught."

"You've been working with Captain Feehan?" she asked incredulously.

"Yeah, I know. You can't quite put it together, right?" Paul's famous smile vanished. "Well, OK, it's not the whole story. I'm not exactly Mr. Law and Order. I was arrested a couple of times two summers ago—petty thievery. Captain Feehan decided to save me from myself. Don't know how he did it, but he did. I might even try to get into the police academy, be a cop for real. What do you think?"

"I think you'd be great at it," Nina said with sincerity. "Especially if they gave you an undercover assignment, and you had to pretend to be a slightly shady playboy type whose only interest—"

"Was kissing beautiful women," Paul finished.

He leaned forward and put his arms around her. His lips grazed hers, then pressed against them, gently urging her lips apart.

"Do you know how long I've wanted to kiss you like that?" he asked when they could bear to pull away from each other.

"Yes," Nina said breathlessly. "I know exactly how long. Because that's how long I've wanted you to kiss me like that."

The woods that had felt so menacing now felt like a magical land. The birds were singing their names. The trees were reaching out to applaud.

"It's too bad we're in a triathlon instead of a kissing competition," Paul said. "Of course, if it were a kissing contest, we'd have to be on the same team."

"Speaking of which—" Nina said reluctantly.

203

"Yeah, I know," Paul answered. "On your mark, get set . . . kiss."

He leaned forward and seized her lips with his own.

"Oh, Paul," Nina murmured.

"I love it when you say my name against my lips." He drew away, his eyes searching hers intently.

"You sound so sad," she whispered. "Are you in pain?"

"I'm sad because I know this is all I'm going to have of you."

A part of her ached to contradict him, to tell him that they could be together forever, but the image of Bryan—strong, loving, counting the seconds until he'd see her again—rose in her mind. This was a day for truth.

"Aren't we lucky just to have a little bit of each other?" she asked softly as he pressed kisses to her cheeks, her chin, her forehead.

"Very lucky. I'll never forget you, Nina Harper." He folded her into his arms. "You're very special."

"So are you."

Over the sound of the trilling birds she thought she heard human voices. If she and Paul didn't make an appearance soon, their teammates were going to send out search parties. Soon the past few moments would be only a very precious memory. Nina decided not to let anyone else ruin it.

She got to her feet and offered Paul a hand up.

"You OK to run?" she asked. "Let me see your head."

The wound wasn't bleeding. Paul would have a bump and maybe a headache, but the small size of his assailant had been to Paul's benefit.

"I think maybe you should check me all over for bruises," Paul said.

"You're OK," she announced crisply.

"Of course, the real bruises can't be seen," he said, his face graver than she'd ever seen it.

"Those bruises will heal too," she said with a sigh. "For both of us."

"But I hope they leave a scar—on the soul," Paul said.

Their eyes locked.

Nina knew that if she didn't tear herself away from Paul now, she never would.

"South Beach, bite my dust!" she called, and slalomed through the trees.

"Sweet Valley Shore, eat your heart out!" Paul rejoined, bolting.

And that's exactly what this Sweet Valley lifeguard will do.

The roar of the crowd was a rhythmic, insistent chant that Wendy seemed to hear with her feet as well as her ears.

"Wen-dy!"

"Ra-chel!"

"Wen-dy!"

"Ra-chel!"

Jaw relaxed, knees to the sky, eyes on the gleaming blue ribbon just another hundred yards ahead.

Her best run ever, she could feel it, but not good enough because Rachel was running even better.

"Wen-dy! Wen-dy!"

"Ra-chel! Ra-chel!"

Once she had found her way back to the trail, she'd made up for lost time with an extra burst of speed. But now she had hit her limit, while Rachel seemed impossibly to have discovered new reserves of strength.

If only it wasn't Rachel to whom she would lose. Wendy still smarted when she thought of Rachel's cruel taunts and of the message she had left for Pedro.

Suddenly a burst of adrenaline surged through Wendy's limbs. She pushed her muscles as hard as she could and felt her strides lengthen as she pounded down the path.

This is one where Rachel's gonna be the loser, Wendy determined.

She pulled abreast of Rachel. Weirdly Rachel seemed to slow down, but Wendy didn't have time to think about what was weird and what was not.

Wendy flew past Rachel and broke through the ribbon at the finish line, the sweat and the tears streaming down her face.

"Yes!" she shouted. "Yes!"

And then she saw him.

She must have died and gone to heaven. Life couldn't be this sweet—but it was.

Pedro was there, throwing his arms around her.

"Wendy, Wendy, my beautiful Wendy, I have missed you so."

"You mean it, Pedro? This was your last fling?" She'd already forgiven him for staying away so long, but she couldn't keep a tremor out of her voice.

"Fling?" He threw back his head and laughed, his earring glinting in the sun. "Well, it rhymes with fling, but it's very different."

"What do you mean?" Wendy asked, suddenly confused.

"The word is *ring*, sweet girl."

Her heart began to pound so fast, she thought she might throw up. "Ring?" she echoed foolishly.

"Yes, I just made a little trip to Mexico. I wanted to surprise you—that's why I didn't call. My grandmother was saving something very important for me—my mother's wedding ring."

Wendy didn't say anything. She could hardly breathe.

"Wendy, I never want to be apart from you again. Will you marry me?"

"Marry you?"

His warm eyes glowed with tenderness. "I've never known anyone like you, Wendy, and I can't risk letting you go." His brow furrowed deeply. "Please tell me your answer quickly."

Wendy flung her arms around Pedro's neck. "Yes! Yes!"

He kissed her and kissed her, and they were surrounded by the crowd's shouts, laughter, and applause as other runners crossed the finish line.

Suddenly he pulled back and began to hum. "Fling . . . ring. I think it's a song," he said. "You don't mind sharing me with my music?" he asked anxiously.

"As long as I don't have to share you with Rachel." Wendy leaned her head against his shoulder in utter contentment.

"Rachel who?" Pedro asked.

"The tall curvy girl who's staring daggers at us," Wendy said. She couldn't repress a touch of smugness. "Along with Tina—she's the Asian girl whose head looks as though it's about to snap off."

"Let's give them something to really stare at," Pedro said mischievously. He bent her backward for a soul-stirring kiss.

They were still kissing when Nina and Paul loped across the finish line about ten minutes later.

Jessica clutched Ben's hand as Captain Feehan swung the bullhorn up to his lips.

Now they would know not only who had won but whether she and Ben would meet again in the fall.

Even before she heard the words, she knew what they would be. Somehow she'd known all along.

"And the winner by one minute and thirty-point-five seconds is . . . *South Beach!*"

Tears began to roll down her cheeks. "Oh no. Oh no." She clutched Ben's arm.

Ben looked as though he wanted to cry himself, but instead he smiled, and this time his lopsided grin was full of pain.

He put his arm around Jessica. "I'll make money as fast as I can," he promised. "And I just know you'll think up something." Cupping her chin, he kissed it tenderly. "I have faith in you to figure out some way of collapsing the miles between us. You'll get them to repeal the laws of physics or something. After all, you're the one with the brains."

Jessica sighed.

She loved his faith in her ingenuity, but she didn't share it.

They were going to have to spend the next four months half a nation apart—and anything might happen in four months.

She almost wished she'd never met the miracle named Ben Mercer.

Nina offered her hand to Rachel. "Congratulations. That was quite a race."

Rachel looked as though she'd been stung. "If there's anything I can't stand, it's a gracious loser," she snarled, turning away.

"Huh?" Nina said.

"Huh?" Paul said.

"Some people just can't stand happiness." Wendy was grinning and dancing around. She could hardly contain her joy.

"Let's all go to Harry's," Winston said. "Win or lose, you gotta have french fries."

Elizabeth and Ryan had the beach to themselves. They sat on the jetty, the surf rolling in softly beneath their feet. Because all the lifeguards had the afternoon off, the No Swimming sign was up, its ropes checked not twice but three times, though Ryan kept scanning the water anyway.

"You're off duty now," she said softly.

For a moment his eyes looked wistful, distant. Then they seemed to clear like clouds suddenly lifting to reveal a clear blue sky.

"It's good to be here with you." He gripped her hand. "I just wish I'd done more for the team."

"You did your best, and your best was pretty wonderful. You made your amends, Ryan. That's the really important thing. And you didn't just make your amends with people," she blurted.

"What do you mean?"

"Looking at you out here I suddenly realized that you and the ocean had to reconcile too. I'm sure you'll find a way."

"Elizabeth—" he began in a choked-up voice, then stopped. "How do you know so much?"

"When you care, you know."

"You never go off duty either," he burst out.

"Look at how you didn't give up on me. How can I possibly pay you back?"

"By never again giving up on yourself," she said. "Will you promise?"

"I promise to try. I can't do more than that."

"That's perfect," she said softly. She leaned back, feeling the rough stone of the jetty beneath her palms and the wind in her hair. As she gazed into Ryan's eyes her lips tingled in expectation.

He kissed her once softly, then dotted her mouth with little kisses. As he pressed kisses against the corners of her lips she dissolved into sugary warmth. Finally his mouth came crashing down against hers in a tide of passion that all but swept her out to sea.

"Ahem, excuse me—"

Their heads flew apart.

One of Captain Feehan's men was writing out a summons.

"What?" Ryan and Elizabeth cried.

"You don't know the law against public displays of affection on Labor Day weekend?" the young officer asked severely. Then he grinned. "Everyone off the beach and up to Harry's for the party. Captain Feehan's orders. And that's for real."

"More fries, Captain Feehan?" Winston asked. "Can I get you salt? Ketchup? Mustard?"

"Heat up your coffee, Captain Feehan?" Harry hovered with the coffeepot. "More sugar? Cream?"

"Relax, boys," the police officer said. He had rarely seemed more relaxed himself. "I know all about your little operation."

Winston dropped the ketchup. Fortunately it was in a plastic squeeze bottle.

Harry's hand shook so badly that coffee sloshed all over the counter.

As Captain Feehan calmly chewed his fry, Winston suppressed a sob. This was it. The end of the world. And it was happening right in the middle of one of the best parties he'd ever gone to. Spirits were outrageously high. Winners and losers alike were giving in to end-of-summer madness, pouring sodas over their heads, running out to the deck to toss bits of roll to the seagulls, clapping and dancing to Harry's retro jukebox.

"What little operation?" Harry finally squeaked.

"How did you know?" Winston asked at the very same moment.

Harry glared at his cohort, but Captain Feehan just laughed.

"I guess you could have hung up a neon sign and put an ad in the papers if you wanted to be *really* obvious, but you sure managed to be conspicuous without them. I've known what you were up to since you took your first bet." He clapped Winston on the back. "If you were looking forward to a life as a criminal, son, I'd suggest that you seek career counseling."

Winston sighed defeatedly. "Thanks."

"But from the look of things, you've already had a change of plans." Captain Feehan's gesture took in Winston's spiffy outfit, from his tie to his shoes. "Looks as though maybe you're thinking of law school—which is a good thing. Every crook should have a lawyer in the family."

Harry finally put down the coffeepot. But he smiled a sickly sweet smile that made Winston feel as though he'd eaten too many glazed doughnuts.

"Gee, Captain Feehan, it's sure a good thing that you're so sophisticated," he began heartily. "We were just having a little fun, livening up the summer for the tourists—but I'm sure I don't have to tell you that, right? I'd bet anything you're one of those enlightened law enforcement people who realize that these victimless crimes just add a little local color to the tourists' summer experience."

Captain Feehan carefully wiped his hands on one of Harry's notoriously skimpy paper napkins. "You'd bet anything, did you say, Harry? And I'd bet that those are the only honest words you've said today. Maybe all year." He shot the restaurant owner a disgusted look. "You even water down the ketchup. Admit it."

Harry stopped smiling. He looked down at the floor.

"I'll get to you guys later," Captain Feehan said in a new, brisk voice. "Right now I've got bigger fish to fry. Did anyone put down an unusually large amount of cash?"

213

Winston and Harry looked at each other. Harry swallowed.

"There was one, um, young adult who was, ah, very persistent." Harry drew a shaky, unhappy-sounding breath, then pointed out the freckle-faced kid.

Winston watched numbly as Captain Feehan walked over to the boy. The boy's friends quickly drew away. Even from across the room Winston could see the pallor beneath the freckles.

"Sis!" the boy cried out, casting frightened eyes toward . . . Rachel!

The laughter stopped.

The conversation died as abruptly as if someone had pulled the plug.

"Rachel?" Winston and Harry chorused.

If the french fries had started to sing and the hamburgers to dance, Winston wouldn't have been surprised. Reality as he knew it had just been stood on its head.

"But why did he bet on Sweet Valley?" Winston asked, his hands palms up in resigned bewilderment.

"Because Rachel told him that South Beach was going to lose!" Elizabeth called out excitedly. "That's why she was so upset with her teammates when they pushed Ben and me!"

"I knew it was too easy to run past her!" Wendy suddenly exclaimed. "I just knew something was wacky."

"And I bet I know who bushwhacked Paul!" Nina exclaimed.

But Paul was already moving toward Rachel's brother, a growl in his throat and menace in his eyes.

Ryan put a powerful hand on Paul's arm. "Aren't you missing the point about who the real culprit is?"

"Traitor!" came the cry from Rachel's squadmate Kristi. "How could you do this?"

An angry murmur rose from the other South Shore lifeguards.

Captain Feehan took a step forward. "Rachel Max, you are under arrest. You are warned that you have the right to remain silent and that any statement you make—"

But as he reached for his handcuffs Rachel streaked by him. Elbowing past the startled onlookers to get to the door, she ran out onto the deck.

Winston felt himself swell up with rage.

Rachel had nearly ruined his life. She'd nearly ruined everybody's life.

He jumped over Harry's counter and dashed across the back room to the window.

"Rachel!" Winston yelled. "Stop her!"

He tugged fruitlessly at the window screen, cemented in place by Harry's greasy fumes. Rachel turned briefly, gave a snort of derisive laughter, and dove into the water.

The hideous thud of a human skull against a wooden post cracked through the silence.

Rachel floated to the surface of the water, face-down.

"Lifeguards!" Winston shouted hysterically. "Help!"

He heard feet thudding in the other room, heard Ryan's clear voice giving orders, but no one else could get to her as quickly as he could.

Every second counted.

Viennese tie, loafers, and all, he kicked through the screen and dove into the frigid water.

Surfacing, he frantically searched the rippling water for Rachel's unconscious body. Her dark form was only a few feet from Winston, but it was bobbing away quickly with the receding tide. With a few quick strokes he reached her, then heaved her over so that she could breathe.

Fairly flying through the water, he towed her toward safety. "Come on, Rachel, breathe!" He was crying. "Breathe!"

He hauled her up onto the pier with help from Ryan and Paul.

"Where were you all summer when we needed you?" Nina scolded, then threw her arms around him. She hugged him as the others cheered and applauded. She solemnly took the lariat holding her silver whistle and placed it around his neck.

Winston was no longer crying. He felt oddly quiet inside.

"Hey, no big deal," he said, peeling off his soggy layers.

Chapter
Fourteen

"Is it going to hurt?" Jessica asked the cute foot doctor.

"It's going to tickle," the doctor said. He looked up from her foot. He suddenly seemed to notice her huge sea green eyes and a heart-shaped face that was surrounded by long golden hair. "Do you like being tickled?" he asked playfully.

An old-style Jessica quip almost popped out— an it-all-depends-on-who's-doing-the-tickling kind of quip. But it didn't come.

Instead her mouth curved in a skewed, sardonic smile that bore a distinct resemblance to Ben's lopsided grin, the one that invariably signaled the coming of Ben's Biting Wit.

"Do you like being kicked?" she asked the doctor.

He didn't say another word as he removed her sutures.

She kept reliving the delicious moment as she drove home. Jessica wasn't ready to swear that she would never, as long as she lived, look at a guy who wasn't Ben. But any other guy would have to have an awful lot going for him. He would have to be more than just another cute doctor, that was for sure.

He would have to write love letters in the sand, make her feel like a cross between Madonna and Madame Curie, kiss the corners of her mouth just so, teach her a new word every day, run like the wind, and, oh yes, know that she *hated* being tickled.

On the way home from the clinic she stopped at Craig's T-Shirt City to pick up her going-away present for Ben. "Is it ready?" she anxiously asked the clerk.

"Hot off the presses," he said as he held it up.

It was a T-shirt she'd had specially printed. On the back was a map of Chicago. On the front was a map of Sweet Valley. Superimposed on the upper left side was the legend *The heart will find the way*.

"Gorgeous!" she exclaimed.

"I hope it does the trick," the clerk pronounced.

"Oh, it will," Jessica said.

Winston kept counting his money. He supposed he'd have bigger wads of bills in his life— he'd better, since he and Denise had already picked out names for their first twelve children—but he doubted that mere dollars would ever mean more to him.

His friends had insisted that he be cut in for a small chunk of their merit pay. He was one of them, after all, not just an honorary member of the lifesaving squad but an honored member. And he deserved more than warm feelings for his heroic rescue of Rachel.

Not that a human life could ever have a dollar value on it. But as Captain Feehan had said, people who make money doing right are less likely to want to make money doing wrong.

The bet had been canceled by order of Captain Feehan. The Sweet Valley gang had all gotten to keep their hard-earned bonuses, and so had the South Beach squad.

Even Rachel got to keep the money she'd honestly earned—which was probably a good thing, all agreed. Her bail bond had been posted at ten thousand dollars. She needed the cash more than anyone else.

On impulse Winston took a fifty-dollar bill, folded a sheet of plain white paper around it, stuck it in an envelope, and addressed it to Rachel at the county jail. After all, in a weird way she'd been responsible for his cleaning up, in every sense of the word.

He dropped the envelope in a mailbox on his way to say good-bye to Wendy.

*   *   *

219

"What are you doing here?" Rachel snarled.

Ben looked at her through the mesh separating the prisoners from their visitors. He felt almost sorry for her. Almost. She looked like a caged creature, a bird of prey that had been trapped and thrown into captivity.

"I came to see if you needed anything," he managed to say.

"Me? Need something? What could I possibly need from you?" Rachel grated sardonically. She gestured at the barren yellow room. There were two other prisoners, women whose hollow eyes and emaciated bodies were eloquent testimony to the treachery of abuse.

"Do you need me to call your parents?" Ben asked.

"Oh, right." Rachel laughed harshly. "If they gave a darn about me, do you think I'd be here now? Go away, Ben. Go back to your fluffy plaything."

He felt his cheeks blaze fire. "Jessica is a wonderful woman."

"I'm afraid I couldn't possibly be less interested in hearing about Jessica. Anyway, I'm sure that after two days back on the campus at Chicago, you'll forget all about her. Can you imagine considering quantum mechanics, Chaucer, and Jessica Wakefield all at the same time? Your brain would implode."

Ben just smiled.

"Yeah, right. Well, I hope you find a branch of

220

Mensa in here, speaking of brains. Let me know if you need a new Scrabble set or anything. Don't forget, *jail* is worth a lot of points if you put the *j* on a triple-letter score. Good-bye, Rachel."

Paul cheered as the machine made the hiccuping sound that meant Nina had won a free game.

"Go, Nina!" He tugged at one of her braids—today festooned with pink and white beads to match the striped shirt she was wearing with crisp white pants and white sandals. Her mother firmly believed that white and pastel clothing had to be put in the cedar closet after Labor Day, and although Nina always teased Mrs. Harper about her rigidity, she tended to follow suit.

They were back in summer fun mode. It was as though they had said all the serious words that needed to be said, and more would only sadden them to no good purpose.

Nina played her free game, then they moved to a table and ordered two papaya-mango-banana smoothies.

Paul raised his glass. "Care to drink to my new life as a police cadet? It's definite. Captain Feehan just told me the good news."

"Congrats!" Nina said with heartfelt warmth. She raised her glass in salute and took a sip.

"So how do you think I'll look in uniform?" Paul's eyes twinkled merrily.

"You're going to have a line this long of gorgeous

221

girls knocking down your door," she said, spreading her hands wide.

"I'd rather have you."

Nina couldn't meet his eyes. "You always will—as a friend," she said lightly.

He groaned. "Your words say one thing, but your kisses sure said another. Which should I believe?"

At the mere mention of kisses, her lips tingled.

"My kisses were real. And so are the words."

He closed his eyes and sighed. Then he flashed his one-and-only smile. "I promise to take your words seriously if you promise to remember the kisses seriously. Deal?"

Nina briefly squeezed his hand. "Paul, a woman would have to have a terminal case of amnesia to forget your kisses. You have yourself a deal."

Winston hugged Wendy, then Pedro, then Paloma. The dignified Carlos resisted a hug, but he offered a paw to shake.

"I can't believe this is good-bye," he said mournfully. "It's been an awesome summer, hasn't it?"

Wendy and Pedro looked at each other.

"Should I ask him now?" Wendy said.

"Why not?" Pedro answered.

Wendy tucked her bare feet under her and cuddled against Pedro. "What are you doing for Halloween?" she asked Winston.

"Halloween?" he echoed. "I have to admit, I hadn't given it much thought. But one thing is sure," he added. "I'm not going to be a hamburger. Why?"

"Well, Pedro and I are thinking of getting married then, and we—"

"Wendy!" He started the hugging all over again. "That's fantastic!"

"I was wondering, would you be my best man?" she asked.

His face felt as if it were going to split, he was grinning so hard. "I'd be thrilled and honored and all those other wonderful things!" he exclaimed. "But I don't have to wear turquoise tulle, do I? Denise hates the way I look in tulle."

"We'll find something else," Wendy promised. "Paloma can wear the tulle."

Winston wiped away a tear. "I guess I'm not a total screwup after all. I mean, you do blame me for being together, don't you?"

"Oh yes," Pedro assured him. "You should hear the things we call you when we have a fight. Though I think I would have found her anyway," he added tenderly. "How could I not have found my Wendy?"

"Easily," Winston said. "You might have been blind and a fool. But luckily you're neither."

Wendy gave him a look he would remember always—tender, grateful, and loving.

Maybe the summer hadn't turned out exactly as Winston had expected—he hadn't made the lifeguard squad, after all. But he'd actually done much better than he had hoped for. He'd made a close friend whom he'd never forget.

"I have a present for you," Jessica announced.

"You do? That's a funny coincidence. I have a present for you," Ben said as he sat on the living-room couch.

"I hope yours is nothing too fancy," Jessica said anxiously. She sat down next to him. "Mine's only a T-shirt."

"That's a very funny coincidence," Ben said. "Mine happens to be a T-shirt too."

"Well, I know one thing," Jessica declared. "The T-shirt you bought me can't possibly be the same as the T-shirt I bought you."

"Oh, really? How do you know?"

"Because I designed yours," Jessica told him proudly. "It's one of a kind. Just like you."

"The one I got for you isn't unique—which isn't to say I don't think you are," Ben replied. "But I admit that mine represents some effort."

"So who's going first?" Jessica asked.

"Ladies first."

Jessica wrinkled her nose. "That's awfully sexist."

"No, just quaint and old-fashioned. OK, men first," Ben said.

"Chauvinist! OK, how about instead of giving each other the tees, we just put them on?" she suggested.

"You mean I put on the one I'm giving you and you put on the one you're giving me?" Ben asked.

"Then mine will smell like you and yours will smell like me," she added with a little sigh. "At least until we wash them."

"We can always mail them back and forth for re-smelling," Ben suggested.

She laughed. "You know what? You're starting to sound more and more like me. I hope they don't think you're an imposter or something when you go back to Chicago."

"I wouldn't worry about that," he said breezily. "OK, here's an idea. We both go to our rooms, put on the shirts we're giving each other, and come back."

"Perfect," Jessica agreed.

"Ready or not," Ben called out a couple of minutes later.

But when she saw the shirt he'd bought for her, she had to bite back her disappointment. It was a UCLA shirt, standard issue, with gold letters on a blue background.

"It's very pretty," she said politely.

He looked at her, the corners of his mouth turning up in the barest suggestion of a held-back grin.

"But why UCLA?" she wondered aloud. She searched her mind for some connection between Ben and the University of California. "I guess it would have been kind of hard to get a University of Chicago tee," she finally said, not wanting to hurt his feelings. "And I bet the colors aren't half as nice."

"Not only hard, it would have been pointless," Ben declared.

"Pointless?" Something was going on, but she didn't get it.

And then she did.

"Ben?"

"Jessica?"

"Are you telling me what I think you're telling me?"

"And what might that be?" he asked solemnly.

"Are you . . . did you . . . is it possible . . ."

"Yes to all the above," Ben said.

Her mouth opened, but no words came out.

"It wasn't easy, but there are some advantages to being a certified genius," he said.

"Ben Mercer, are you really and truly telling me that you have transferred from the University of Chicago to UCLA?" Jessica squealed.

"It's not definite yet, but I'm really going to try to make it happen," Ben said.

"Oh, Ben," Jessica said. "How incredible."

"Which is not a bad way of describing your T-shirt," Ben said. "Especially with you in it."

Jessica looked down at her own chest. "I guess it's a little beside the point now."

"'The heart will find the way,'" Ben read aloud. "That's hardly beside the point. It's exactly the point. As usual."

226

Jessica sighed rapturously. "UCLA. That's practically around the corner from SVU. You know, if you're not careful, I might get the idea that you like me."

"Jumping to conclusions again, Jess," he said in a cautionary voice.

"Yes, I could definitely begin to believe it," she said.

"Well, don't ever believe it too absolutely," he teased. "Because one of the funnest things in the whole world is trying to prove it to you."

"Do they allow you to say *funnest* at Mensa meetings?" she asked.

"Not for a minute. But at UCLA even the professors say it. Do you think our shirts would smell too much like each other if we brought them a little closer?"

"I think we owe it to science to find out," Jessica averred solemnly.

Ben said he quite agreed.

Elizabeth had a rule about packing. Never pack at one end of a trip what you don't want to have to unpack at the other end.

She went through all her pockets. She carefully emptied her shoulder bags of used tissues, souvenir matchbooks she would never use and didn't want to hoard, a playbill from a summer stock production better forgotten, a beach stone she'd once thought beautiful.

The stone had a thin band of white that encircled it. Someone had told her that a wish might be made on such a stone. But the wish would come true only if you gave away the stone.

She made a wish. That Ryan would make peace with the ocean and with himself.

She walked down to the beach and gave the stone back to the sea. She hurled it into the water near the jetty where she and Ryan had kissed the day of the triathlon.

Ryan was sitting on the sand in front of her beach house, even though the sky was thick with clouds and the beach was officially closed. She saw him shifting restlessly, and she knew he was hoping against hope that somehow, miraculously, time would spin backward, and this time the sea would give back the child alive.

Yet his face had a tranquil cast to it, and she knew he was truly healing, making his final amends. He couldn't stop hoping for a miracle, but at the same time he knew the hope for what it was—an impossible dream.

And that was what they had been. A dream she would always be glad she had dreamt and yet one she would always be glad had never been fully realized.

He caught sight of her. "Elizabeth. I was just coming to see you. All packed up?"

"Just about."

"I'll help you load the Jeep." He walked up to meet her.

"Thanks. Actually, I've got something for you.

I made a big batch of brownies for you to take to your next meeting."

"That was really sweet of you," he said.

"Will you always have to go to meetings?" she asked.

"Probably," he said. "I can't take any chances. Drinking has cost me so much." He took her hand, and their arms swung easily between them. "You, for instance."

"I'm still so glad we met," she burst out. "Aren't you?"

"Of course. I just wish it happened a couple of years sooner. But it didn't, did it?"

She shook her head. "Are you going to be all right?"

"I think I will be in time."

"Oh, Ryan." She closed her eyes against the pain she heard in his voice—the pain she couldn't touch. She thought of all the nights he would spend by himself while she was back among her friends at SVU, back in Tom's loving arms.

"You won't be lonely?" she asked anxiously.

"I'll be fine. I have lots to do. Some night when it's perfectly clear, I'm going to find a new constellation and name it for you."

Elizabeth's eyes glowed.

"Something at the far edge of the Milky Way—almost but not quite out of sight."

"Ryan." She sighed. "Ryan, Ryan." For a long moment it was enough to say his name, and then it wasn't enough.

He took her in his arms. He kissed her and held her tightly.

The kisses were different this time. They thrilled her and saddened her at the same time.

It felt as if Ryan were trying to memorize her lips, and she knew why.

These kisses were going to have to last a lifetime.

When they broke apart, she didn't know whether the wetness on her cheeks came from his tears or her own or maybe both.

What happens to the hunks of Sweet Valley Shore when Elizabeth, Nina, and Jessica return to SVU? Find out more about Ryan, Paul, and Ben next summer in another three-part lifeguard miniseries. (Coming in June, July, and August of 1997)

SIGN UP FOR THE SWEET VALLEY HIGH® FAN CLUB!

Hey, girls! Get all the gossip on Sweet Valley High's® most popular teenagers when you join our fantastic Fan Club! As a member, you'll get all of this really cool stuff:

- Membership Card with your own personal Fan Club ID number
- A Sweet Valley High® Secret Treasure Box
- Sweet Valley High® Stationery
- Official Fan Club Pencil (for secret note writing!)
- Three Bookmarks
- A "Members Only" Door Hanger
- Two Skeins of J. & P. Coats® Embroidery Floss with flower barrette instruction leaflet
- Two editions of *The Oracle* newsletter
- Plus exclusive Sweet Valley High® product offers, special savings, contests, and much more!

- -

Be the first to find out what Jessica & Elizabeth Wakefield are up to by joining the Sweet Valley High® Fan Club for the one-year membership fee of only $6.25 each for U.S. residents, $8.25 for Canadian residents (U.S. currency). Includes shipping & handling.

Send a check or money order (do not send cash) made payable to "Sweet Valley High® Fan Club" along with this form to:

SWEET VALLEY HIGH® FAN CLUB, BOX 3919-B, SCHAUMBURG, IL 60168-3919

NAME_____
(Please print clearly)

ADDRESS_____

CITY_____ STATE_____ ZIP_____
(Required)

AGE_____ BIRTHDAY_____ /_____ /_____